BEATRIX THE BOLD

and the
RIDDLE TOWN
DRAGON

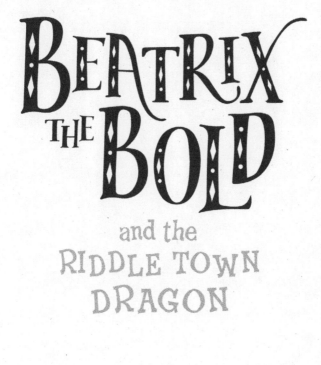

BEATRIX
THE BOLD

and the
RIDDLE TOWN
DRAGON

Simon
Mockler

Piccadilly
PRESS

First published in Great Britain in 2019 by
PICCADILLY PRESS
80–81 Wimpole St, London W1G 9RE
www.piccadillypress.co.uk

A CIP catalogue record for this book is available from the British
Library.

ISBN: 978-1-848-12767-8
also available as an ebook

1
Printed and bound in Great Britain by Clays Ltd, Elcograf S.p.A.

Piccadilly Press is an imprint of Bonnier Books UK
www.bonnierbooks.co.uk

For Penelope and Louis

Prologue

Ladies and gentlemen, mums and dads, boys and girls, little brothers and older sisters, small pets, large pets, dogs, hamsters, cats and cross-eyed pigeons, welcome to the second story in the life of young Queen. For those of you who haven't read the first book, I'll tell you quickly what happened. If you've read the first book, please feel free to skip this bit. Although if you do, you will miss a *very* good joke about carrots which wasn't actually in the first book, so if you like jokes, or if you just like carrots, you should have a read.

Right, here we go.

There was a young queen called Beatrix but she didn't know she was a queen and she lived in secret in a palace with her Aunt Esmerelda and Uncle Ivan. Her aunt was mean and her uncle didn't like children or jokes, so when Beatrix said things like, 'What did one snowman say to the other snowman?... Can you smell carrots?' he'd throw a knife at the wall. Once it very nearly hit Esmerelda and would have killed her stone dead if

she hadn't ducked to pick up a shiny gold coin she'd just seen on the floor.

It wouldn't have mattered too much if he had killed her because Esmerelda was incredibly evil and actually it might have saved a lot of trouble for poor Beatrix, but it would have been a completely different story, with a different name (probably something like *The World's Deadliest Joke*), and Uncle Ivan would have ended up in prison, but none of that happened.

What did happen was that Esmerelda told the Evil Army from Beyond the Woods to kidnap Beatrix so that she would get lots and lots of gold, but Beatrix defeated the army with the help of her friends disguised as Wobblers.

What's a Wobbler? Wobblers are mythical creatures that hide in the woods and gobble up children. They're mean. They're dangerous. They're *angry*. That's why the Evil Army ran away when they saw Beatrix and her friends disguised as them.

What else happened in the first book? Oh yes, Beatrix met Oi the boy and Dog 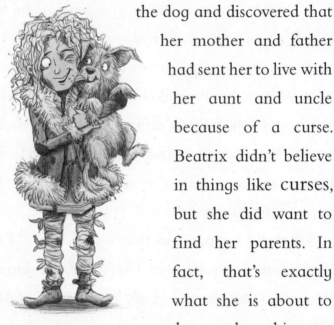 the dog and discovered that her mother and father had sent her to live with her aunt and uncle because of a curse. Beatrix didn't believe in things like curses, but she did want to find her parents. In fact, that's exactly what she is about to do — today, this very instant. She's just waiting for Wilfred the Wise to find the map that shows the way, then she's going to pack her bags and get ready for the journey, a journey so dangerous she'll need a disguise, some magic tricks and at least three spare pairs of underpants.

1

The Map

It was early morning in the middle of January and the air was as cold and crisp as a – well, as a cheese and onion crisp. The golden palace at the end of Numb Butt Lane was covered in a layer of soft white snow that looked like melted marshmallow. In the kitchens the cooks were baking a fresh batch of fartinpants to warm everyone up and the hot fires sent thick, smoky burps through the chimneys into the bright blue sky.

Deep in the tunnels under the palace, Wilfred the Wise was searching through dusty boxes for a map, a map that showed the way to the castle Beatrix's mother and father lived in. He was sure it was there somewhere, because he'd put it in the box that held all his magic tricks many years ago, on the

very night the young queen had arrived at the palace. Problem was, he couldn't find the box. He had found three dusty gobstoppers, a tiny jumping frog from a Christmas cracker and seven foreign coins, but he hadn't found the map.

He was down to his last half a candle when he finally found the box he wanted. He opened it.

There, underneath a pair of very large magician's underpants with seven hidden compartments, was a scroll of thick parchment.

He unrolled it and looked at the route they needed to take. His hands were trembling. You could see the badly-drawn Wobblers in the spooky woods. You could see the Evil Army's castle. You could see the river that flowed fast from the high mountains. He drew a deep breath. Just looking at the map made him feel nervous.

Outside in the palace courtyard, Queen Beatrix and Oi the boy were wrapped up in furs and making the most of the snow.

'How much longer do you think Wilfred will be?' Oi said.

'Who knows? There are a lot of secret passages under the palace. He's got a lot of places to look. Right, there we go,' Beatrix said, adding the final touches to her snowman. It was most impressive.

A snow soldier – complete with shield, helmet and some old clothes she'd borrowed from Uncle Ivan. She stood back to have a look at her work.

'Well,' she said. 'I think that looks pretty good. Even if I do say so myself.'

'Not bad,' Oi said. 'Not bad at all. Of course, a snow soldier is really just for beginners.'

'Beginners?' Beatrix said, surprised. 'No it's not. It's very difficult to make a snowman look like a vicious soldier. And this one looks almost as vicious as Uncle Ivan.'

'That's because you've used his clothes and armour. For a real challenge, to show you're a real master of snow sculpture, you should try to make these.' Oi pointed at a wooden log with some snow on it.

'Ta-dah!' he said, smiling like a magician who's just made a tiger disappear.

'You made a log?' Beatrix said, staring at the log.

'Not the log. Look at what's on top of it,'

he said. Beatrix stared. She still couldn't see anything except a few snowy dots.

'I don't get it,' she said, starting to feel a little impatient and rather cold. Every so often she got a waft of fresh fartinpants from the kitchens and it made her tummy rumble.

'Look. There. On the log. Snow *ants*.' He pointed at the trail of tiny dots on the log. 'You see, anyone can make a great big snowman – the real skill is making something tiny.'

Beatrix stared at him, not sure if he was joking. She knelt down and looked at the tiny snow balls arranged neatly on the log. Each one was no bigger than half a jelly bean.

'Snow ants are much harder to make than snowmen,' said Oi. 'My brothers always said snowmen were too easy and I was the best at making snow ants.'

'Hmm,' said Beatrix. 'These were the same brothers who told you to guard a field of mud, weren't they?'

Oi shrugged. 'Look at this…' He used a leaf to scoop up a snow ant. It had blades of grass for its legs, two threads of moss for its antennae and a teeny tiny smile he'd made by pressing his little fingernail gently into its head.

'That's pretty good,' Beatrix said. 'Actually, I think I can say it's the best snow ant I've ever seen. I mean, it's certainly the *first* snow ant I've ever seen.'

'BEATRIX!!!'

They both ducked. It was Uncle Ivan. There was something about his booming voice that made you duck whenever you heard it.

'WHERE ARE MY CLOTHES?!! WHERE'S MY ARMOUR??!!!'

His voice echoed round the courtyard. Two icicles that were hanging from the roof broke off and smashed to the ground.

'Oh dear,' Beatrix said quietly. 'He sounds extremely grumpy.'

Uncle Ivan stormed down the palace steps into the courtyard. Even though he was wearing pyjamas and a dressing gown, he still had one of his knives tucked into his belt. His hand was hovering over the handle, which was never a good sign.

'WHY IS THAT SNOWMAN WEARING MY CLOTHES??!!'

Beatrix really wanted to say, *Because he's cold*, but she didn't. Instead she said: 'Sorry, Uncle Ivan.

They were lying on the floor outside your room and looked quite old and were a little bit, er, well, a little bit stinky. I thought you'd thrown them away.'

'They're not old and they don't smell!' Ivan bellowed. 'I had a bath a month ago and I put on a new pair of underpants just before we fought the Evil Army last year. Surely you know that's my favourite outfit.' Ivan's fists were clenched. He pulled back his arm, as if he was about to punch the poor snowman in the head, when something made him stop suddenly.

'Ooh, look at these snow ants,' he said, bending down and looking at the log. 'Very fine detailing. Who did these?'

'I did,' Oi replied.

'Well done, Oi – I haven't seen skill like this before. Quite remarkable. You could learn a thing or two here, young Beatrix. Now, let's get inside. Wilfred has found the map.'

2

Beatrix the Boy

Wilfred the Wise, Oi the boy, Dog the dog and Beatrix the Bold sat round the enormous table in the palace dining room. Ivan the Vicious was still in his pyjamas, and stood in front of the fireplace, munching on a fartinpant. Wilfred had placed the map in the centre of the table so they could all see it.

'Right,' Wilfred said. 'This will show us the way to your parents' castle in Beluga, Beatrix. It's a very dangerous journey. There are two ways

to get there – one is by sailing over the Sea of Sinking Ships; the other is over land, crossing the mountains. If we go by ship it'll be faster, but the ship may well sink and we might all drown. I wouldn't recommend it. The route through the mountains is also dangerous, and we'd have to complete it in two weeks – before the ice thaws and the avalanches start – but we definitely won't drown. So, on balance, given the risk of drowning versus the risk of avalanches, I'd suggest we cross the mountains.'

Beatrix looked at the map.

'There's not much information, is there?' she said. 'There are a lot of warning signs. Some fields. But other than that it's just arrows and some very simple drawings of flowers. And what looks like a big bar of chocolate over here. Where's the danger?' she said.

'Hang on,' Wilfred replied. 'You're looking at it upside down.' He spun the map around.

'These flowers are supposed to be Wobblers that live in the woods. I agree they're not very good drawings of Wobblers, but then no one really knows what a Wobbler looks like, do they?'

He dipped his quill in ink and drew a snout and some sharp teeth onto the Wobblers.

'There. That's better,' he said. 'The thing that looks like a big bar of chocolate is actually General Burpintime's castle. The Evil Army still want to capture you. They think you're going to take over their kingdom and destroy them. And Esmerelda will want revenge. She doesn't have any gold any more, and that's going to make her angry. Extremely angry. Who knows, maybe she's already teamed up with General Burpintime.'

Uncle Ivan's face grew red as he heard this, and before you could say, *Don't throw a knife at the wall, it'll only make a hole in the wood*, he'd thrown a knife at the wall and split the wood panelling.

'Well, we'll have the perfect disguise,' said

Beatrix. 'A family of travelling magicians on our way to Beluga. With your tricks, and with me and Oi as your assistants, no one will suspect a thing. What else do we need to watch out for? It looks like there's a drawing of something here, by the bend in the river. It's a bit smudgy, but it looks like…' She spun the map around. 'A snake that's eaten a Christmas tree?'

'Can't be,' Wilfred replied. 'There are no snakes that far north, it's too cold.' He frowned. 'I think it's the ancient symbol for a dragon,' he said. 'Now, why would they have drawn a dragon here?' He stroked his beard. 'I feel like I should know the answer to this one… no. It's gone. Oh well, if you can't remember something, then it's probably not important, as my old headmaster used to say. At least I think he said that. I can't remember. What *is* important, is that we have some good disguises to stop anyone recognising us, and of course I need to teach you and Oi some basic magic so you can help me with any tricks we need to perform.'

'You're sure there's no dragon?' Oi said.

'One hundred per cent sure – because dragons don't actually exist. Right, who wants to try on disguises and learn some magic?'

'I do!' Beatrix said. 'Let's go to the story room – it has all sorts of costumes.'

Beatrix, Oi and Wilfred rummaged through cupboards in the story room, looking for costumes and props they could use as disguises.

'I'm going to dress up as a boy,' Beatrix said, pulling out a cape and a pair of baggy trousers.

'*I am a boy*,' she said in a deep voice. Then again, in a slightly lower voice, '*I am a boy*.'

'Um, boys don't go round saying, *I am a boy*,' Oi said. 'Because, you know, they already are boys.'

'Of course I know that! If I was a boy I'd say things like, *Kissing is gross* and *Would you rather have a pet T-Rex or a pet crocodile?*'

'What's this?' Wilfred said, pulling what looked like a squirrel's tail out of the chest.

'A fake beard!' said Beatrix. 'I'm definitely trying this on.' She hooked the beard around her ears, and pressed it onto her chin.

'How do I look?' she said, once again using her deepest voice. She placed her hands on her hips.

'I think that's the weirdest thing I've ever seen,' Oi replied.

 'You certainly don't look like Beatrix the Bold any more,' Wilfred said. He took a pointy hat from the chest and gave it to her. Beatrix put it on, and stuffed a pillow under her tunic so she had a big belly.

'I'm *Fernando the Fantastic*,' she said, swirling her cape. The hat fell off. 'I think I'll save this one for emergencies. The beard is very itchy.'

Oi put on a fake nose. 'And I am the boy with the unbelievable sense of smell. So strong he can sniff out a sprout from half a mile away. Then run half a mile in the opposite direction. They call me *Norman the Nose*.'

Wilfred looked through the chest.

'Shall I just be Wilfred the Wise? It's not like anyone is looking for me. And I'm already a magician.'

'You should at least have a different name,' said Beatrix.

'How about...'

'Bob!' Oi said.

'Bob the Magician?' Wilfred stroked his beard. 'I suppose it'll be easy to remember. You can be Norman; I'll be Bob; Beatrix, how about we call you...'

'Harry?' Beatrix suggested. 'It's a great name for someone who's training to be a magician.'

'Harry?' Wilfred repeated. 'I don't think I've ever met a magician called Harry.'

'I'll be the first, and I'm sure I won't be the last. If I talk in a deep voice, wear those funny trousers and keep a hat on over my hair no one will know I'm a girl.'

'Well, technically you should have a bit more mud on you,' Oi said. 'But basically, that's all there is to it. Trousers, hat, mud, talking boy stuff and – boom, you're a boy.'

Once they had chosen their disguises, Wilfred opened his box of magic tricks. He showed them how to make a coin go through a plate, how to hide cards up your sleeve, and even how to escape from chains using a special padlock with a secret button hidden underneath. Beatrix and Oi practised the tricks, then they packed everything away in a big wooden box, ready to load onto the cart.

It was a lot of fun, but Beatrix couldn't help thinking that the only reason they needed the tricks and the disguises was because the Evil Army would be looking for her. It wouldn't be as much fun performing the tricks if their lives depended on it.

3

Esmerelda the Terrible
and General Burpintime

Wilfred the Wise was right when he said that Esmerelda was probably up to something already, and he was right when he said she was probably up to that something with General Burpintime.

If you've read the first book, you'll already know quite a lot about Queen Beatrix's aunt, Esmerelda the Terrible. You'll know that she ran away from the palace once her plan to get the

Evil Army to kidnap Queen Beatrix had failed. You'll know that she loved gold, and that she was mostly incredibly mean, but was occasionally kind, which made her meanness all the more confusing.

Whilst Oi, Wilfred and Beatrix were getting ready to start their journey, Esmerelda the Terrible was sitting opposite General Burpintime in the dining hall of his castle. It had taken her three days to get there. She'd had to steal a horse, climb a mountain and run away from a very angry cat.

'So, Esmerelda,' General Burpintime said. 'Your plan to help us kidnap Queen Beatrix didn't exactly work out well, did it?'

General Burpintime was sitting upon a *very* high chair at the head of the table. His little legs didn't quite reach the ground, and Esmerelda couldn't help thinking he looked like a baby in a high chair. He had a large bowl of marshmallows beside him and managed to keep talking while he ate them.

'My plan was perfect,' Esmerelda said, angrily. 'It was your fear of Wobblers that meant it didn't work. If you and your army hadn't run away in the middle of the night you could have caught Beatrix the next day, given me my gold and got on with doing whatever it is an Evil Army does.'

'Fear of Wobblers?! Don't be so ridiculous.' General Burpintime paused. *Gulp*. He swallowed a marshmallow whole, his eyes bulged and his face turned red. Esmerelda was about to get up and whack him on the back when he coughed. A big blobby white thing appeared on his lips. He took it out, inspected it, then popped it back in his mouth and ate it. Esmerelda felt a little bit of sick rise in the back of her throat. Gross.

'You were saying?' Esmerelda said.

'I was saying I am not afraid of Wobblers. Now, tell me what you want.'

Esmerelda got up and walked around the table. She stood very close to General Burpintime.

'Gold,' she said in a very low voice. 'I want gold, and I want *revenge*.'

General Burpintime grabbed another handful of marshmallows.

'Revenge on Queen Beatrix?' he said.

'Of course! If it wasn't for her escaping, I wouldn't have lost everything. All my gold, my palace, my fifty-two pairs of golden underpants.'

General Burpintime stopped eating marshmallows. He was puzzled by Esmerelda. After all, it had been her idea to try and get the Evil Army to kidnap Beatrix. He wasn't sure you could take revenge because someone had simply escaped when you tried to kidnap them. What else were they meant to do?!

Although he didn't want to tell her, it really was all her fault that she'd lost her gold. And her palace. And her underpants. She was basically a bit greedy, he thought, as he shoved another handful of marshmallows in his mouth. Still, there might be something in this for him.

'I have a proposal,' he said at last. 'I still need to find Beatrix and kill her – because the Curse of the Wobblers isn't going to go away until we do.

If we don't stop her, she'll lead an army of Wobblers to destroy the Evil Army, but...' He popped another marshmallow in his mouth. They helped him concentrate. 'Maybe you can help me, and I can help you. I'll give you gold.'

'How much gold?'

'Lots. Let's worry about the details later,' he said, waving his hand. 'What's more important is that you help me capture Queen Beatrix.'

'How much gold?'

'Um.' General Burpintime paused. In a way, it didn't matter what he said, because he wasn't actually planning to give Esmerelda any gold, even if she did help him. But giving away imaginary gold was almost as hard for him as giving away real gold.

'A whole carriage full,' he said at last. 'A big carriage. Deal?'

General Burpintime held out his hand. Esmerelda got up and shook it. It was like shaking hands with a melted marshmallow. All warm and sticky. Possibly the worst handshake ever.

'Deal,' she said. She patted Burpintime on the back, as if to say, *Good show, all agreed*, but really she was wiping the marshmallow off her hand and onto Burpintime's fur cape.

'I know exactly where she'll be going,' Esmerelda said. 'Now the secret's out, and she knows she's Queen of Beluga, she'll be on her way there. She'll want to see her parents, and I imagine she'll also want to start being queen – queening about the place. Bossing everyone around. Bring me a map so I can work out which route she's likely to take. And bring me an artist. I'll describe Beatrix to them

so they can draw her – that way your spies will have a picture of her.'

'Very well,' General Burpintime said. He clapped his hands together to call for a servant. '*Bring me a map and an artist!*' he shouted. There was no response. His voice echoed around the room. He sat in silence and fished about for another marshmallow.

'You do know it's only us in here, don't you?' Esmerelda said, after what seemed like a very long time.

'Of course I do,' General Burpintime replied in a very irritable voice. He climbed down from his high chair, stamped out of the room and slammed the door behind him. Esmerelda waited, then waited some more. She took a couple of marshmallows and popped them into her mouth, carefully re-arranging the rest so it looked as if none had been taken.

A few moments later General Burpintime

returned with a map and an artist. The artist was dressed in a black cape, with a black beret on his head and white hair poking out underneath. He had a very serious expression.

'This is my own personal artist,' General Burpintime said. 'He's currently painting a series of pictures of giant marshmallows for me, but he's kindly agreed to help us.'

'Can you draw people?' Esmerelda said.

The artist shrugged. 'Of course I can, but I don't like to. It's too… *obvious*,' he said, mysteriously. He placed a piece of paper and some charcoal on the table. 'Describe her and I will draw her.'

'OK, let's see,' Esmerelda said. 'Beatrix is very annoying, and rather spoilt. She tells terrible jokes, like, *What's a duck's favourite food? Biscuits* – I think that was how it went. And she's small. Well, not small for a child. But smaller than a grown-up. And her clothes are very expensive, with jewels and bright colours. But she might be in disguise, so she may just be wearing something boring and normal-looking. And she is always asking questions...'

Esmerelda stopped talking and stared at the blank piece of paper.

'Why haven't you drawn anything?' she said.

'Because you haven't told me what she looks like!' the artist replied. 'What colour hair does she have? Are her eyes big or small? Does her chin stick out? Has it got a dimple? What about freckles?'

'Oh I see, yes, well. Beatrix is…' Esmerelda frowned. It was a lot harder to describe Beatrix than she'd thought it would be.

In the end, the artist produced a drawing that looked like Beatrix reflected in the back of a spoon. Her face was wide in the middle and thin at the top. He'd got the hair right though. There was a mass of curls on top of her head, more than enough for two robins, a starling and a baby barn owl to hide in.

General Burpintime looked at the picture a little doubtfully. 'What a strange-looking niece you have, Esmerelda. I'll give this to my spies. If they see anyone that looks a bit like an egg, I'll make sure they arrest them.'

'It's better than nothing,' Esmerelda said. 'Now, give me the map and I'll tell you where I think she's going.'

General Burpintime unrolled the map on the table. Esmerelda looked at it closely. 'I don't think she'll travel over the Sea of Sinking Ships, not at this time of year. Too dangerous. I think she'll come this way, over the mountains. And she'll have to leave soon – she can't cross the mountains in the spring because of the avalanches, so make sure you send some spies to watch the palace as soon as you can. Put them along Numb Butt Lane and at any inns along the way. Beatrix will need to stop for food. Do all that and you'll catch her easily. Then you can give me my gold. Lots of gold.'

'Of course I will,' General Burpintime said.

'Yes, you will,' Esmerelda replied. 'That's what we agreed.'

'That's why I said it.'

'Good.'

'Good.'

General Burpintime looked at Esmerelda. Esmerelda looked at General Burpintime. Neither blinked. Neither looked away. And neither one trusted the other.

4

A Cross-eyed Present

Beatrix hardly slept a wink that night. She was feeling nervous about the trip, but it wasn't because of the danger. She hadn't seen her parents since she was a few weeks old, and she couldn't remember them at all. Whenever she thought about this, her feelings became all jumbled up in her tummy, as if she'd squidged tomato sauce onto her porridge instead of syrup.

Uncle Ivan had given her a painting of them

from many years ago and hung it on the wall in her room. She got out of bed, wrapped her blanket around her shoulders and looked at it.

Her dad wasn't a fierce warrior like Uncle Ivan – he was actually quite small, but he had a twinkle in his clever eyes and his mouth turned upward in one corner as if he'd thought of something a bit funny and a bit naughty. Beatrix thought that must be a good thing. Uncle Ivan had told her that her dad was always telling jokes – and it looked as if he was about to make one right there in the picture.

Her mother was taller than her father and beautiful with very curly hair, just like her. There were all sorts of flowers woven into her dress and bright jewels around her neck. She wasn't smiling, but somehow she still looked happy.

BOOM BOOM BOOM!

Beatrix jumped. The knocks at the door sounded like a battering ram. *Uncle Ivan*, she thought.

No one else could make that much noise with just their hand and a wooden door, apart from, maybe, a very impatient gorilla desperate for the loo. She opened the door.

'Hullo,' he said. 'I thought I saw a light. I can't sleep either. Are you all right?'

'Yes, I'm fine,' Beatrix said, although the porridge with tomato sauce feeling was still in her tummy.

'Good good,' Uncle Ivan said, looking round the room. 'It'll be strange here without you. A lot quieter of course. But very strange too.' There was a funny look in his eye, as if he had something in it, and was trying to blink it away.

'Would you like a handkerchief?' she said.

'*Me?* No, I'm fine too,' Uncle Ivan sniffed. 'We're all fine. That's good.' He paused, then said: 'You know, your mother and father might expect you to stay with them and be Queen of Beluga, ruling the land. They might want you to stay there for ever. And you would have to. You couldn't just come back. A queen has to look after her people.'

'I know,' Beatrix said, realising she didn't know anything at all about being queen and ruling a land and all the people in it. Surely they had some kind of book or instruction guide that told you how to do it?

There was another knock on the bedroom door. Beatrix opened it. Mrs Fartinpants stood there with a tray. On it was a jug of warm milk and honey and a plate of fresh fartinpants with golden syrup.

'I thought I heard voices,' she

said. 'No doubt you'll be wanting a little late-night snack?'

'Yes please!' Beatrix said, wondering if there'd be someone as nice as Mrs Fartinpants at her parents' castle.

'Here, look – I've made you something,' Mrs Fartinpants said. She gave Beatrix a large hat she'd knitted herself. It looked a bit like the top of a toadstool. Beatrix wasn't sure how much she wanted to look like a walking toadstool, but she thought it was nice of Mrs Fartinpants to make it for her.

'It'll keep you nice and warm,' Mrs Fartinpants said, 'and it's so big no one will be able to see your face under it, so it's a good disguise too.'

'Thank you,' Beatrix said. She tried on the hat, feeling very much like a giant toadstool.

'Now, there's one last thing,' Uncle Ivan said. 'Come with me. You'll need your fur coat. I have something to show you. Something very important to me.'

Uncle Ivan led Beatrix through the twisting, turning corridors of the palace, all the way to his falconry. The falconry was where he kept the eagles he used for hunting. It was a huge cage made from carved wooden pillars. Beatrix was excited. Uncle Ivan was going to give her one of his magnificent birds to take with her!

'Here you are,' he said, passing her a small cage with a pigeon in it. 'He's called Jeff,' Ivan said proudly.

'Jeff?' Beatrix replied, feeling a little disappointed.

'Yes, Jeff the pigeon. He may not look it, but Jeff is one of my best birds. No matter where you are, he will always fly home. If ever you're in danger and you need help, write a message and Jeff will deliver it to me, won't you, my boy?' Ivan said. Jeff cooed. He looked slightly cross-eyed.

'Thank you,' Beatrix said, wondering how long it would take a pigeon to fly all the way back to the palace. And how often Uncle Ivan checked his birdcage for messages. It wasn't exactly WhatsApp.

5

The Journey Begins

It took Beatrix, Wilfred and Oi another day to get everything ready for their journey. They packed a tent, ropes for climbing, dry wood for fires and candles. They packed blankets and warm clothes, a very large supply of sweets and, of course, a big box of magic tricks, just in case they had to prove they really *were* a family of travelling magicians.

They loaded everything onto their cart. It had a cover that stretched over a wooden frame to keep the rain and snow off, a bit like a small caravan. On the side of it they'd painted the words *Bob the Magician's Amazing Magic Show* in gold paint. (There were still a few pots in the palace, even though Esmerelda was no longer there.)

Ivan had given them one of his strongest and most reliable horses to pull them along.

'Jeff will look after you,' Uncle Ivan said.

'Jeff?' Beatrix said. 'Same as Jeff the pigeon?'

Uncle Ivan shrugged. 'I like the name. And besides, no one's going to confuse a pigeon with a horse.'

'Suppose not,' Beatrix said. 'But that does explain why I saw Oi trying to attach the reins to a pigeon earlier. I think we should leave in secret while it's still dark. Oi and I will hide amongst the bags in the back of the cart until we're a good distance away.'

Beatrix was right to be worried. The spy sent by General Burpintime and Esmerelda was

watching the palace from Numb Butt Lane. He was disguised as a snowman. He was cold and he was bored and he was definitely the grumpiest-looking snowman you've ever seen.

When he saw a cart leave the palace, bouncing along the bottom-numbing road in the dark, he didn't think anything of it. He could see a man sitting in the front, and he could just about make out the writing on the side that said *Bob the Magician's Amazing Magic Show*, but he couldn't see a girl with lots of curly hair who looked like an egg, and he couldn't see anyone wearing fancy colourful clothes with lots of jewels. He watched it go by then went back to pretending to be a snowman, wishing he was doing his spying inside a nice warm inn, instead of outside in the freezing cold.

Beatrix, Oi and Wilfred didn't notice the snowman. In fact, for the first ten miles of their journey they didn't notice anything much at all. That's because there was nothing much to notice. Just snow and ice and empty fields and trees with no leaves and nothing really happening apart from Jeff the horse making lots of snorty noises as he pulled the cart. For the next ten miles, nothing happened again, and for the third ten miles, nothing kept happening all the time.

Beatrix, Oi and Wilfred played I-spy for a bit. They ate three and a half bags of sweets and then felt a bit sick. They played noughts and crosses, hangman and battleships, but mostly they just trundled along the

snowy ground wishing they'd brought an extra cushion for the seats.

'How long till we get there?' Oi said.

'Another two weeks!' Wilfred said. 'Same as when you last asked. And we have to hurry – we can't risk the snow melting and the start of the avalanches in the mountains. If we can't cross the mountains in time we'll have to wait till the end of spring, or take our chances on the Sea of Sinking Ships.'

'*Two more weeks*,' Oi said under his breath. He gave a low whistle and drummed his fingers on the side of the cart. He looked thoroughly bored. Almost as bored as Dog, who was usually quite happy hanging his head over the side of the cart and letting the wind flap his ears. The only passenger who didn't look bored was Jeff the pigeon. Jeff was making little cooing noises as if this was the most exciting thing that had ever happened to him.

'I spy with my little eye…' Beatrix said, then she stopped. 'Oh look, an inn. Hooray! Let's stop for lunch.'

In the distance was a log hut with a thatched roof. Smoke was rising out of the chimney. It was a most welcome sight. There was a barn for the horses and a small courtyard with quite a lot of carts in it. Some carts had parked but others seemed to have formed a queue and would stop outside a window, pick up their food and then drive off without even getting out.

As they approached, they saw a big 'M' hanging from a post outside.

'This must be one of those new squashed-meatball-and-bread-rolls places Mr McDonald has opened up,' said Beatrix.

The only parking space left was very small and it took Wilfred three attempts to steer the cart into it. This was because a large, four-wheel drive carriage had parked very badly, taking up two spaces.

'Hang on,' said Wilfred. 'It does seem very busy,' he went on. 'I know that everyone loves a squashed-meatball-and-bread-roll, but all the same, let's be careful. Now, do you remember who you are?'

'We're travelling magicians,' Oi said.

'Good, and what are we not?'

'We're not helping Queen Beatrix travel in secret to find her parents.'

'SHHHHHHH!' said Beatrix. 'Someone might hear. Let's bring Dog and Jeff with us so they can warm up – they look half frozen.'

'We can't bring a horse into the inn,' Oi said. 'They have rules about that kind of thing.'

'Not Jeff the horse. Jeff the pigeon. I knew having

two Jeffs would cause problems,' she muttered to herself. 'Where's that hat Mrs Fartinpants gave me?'

Oi, Dog, Jeff, Beatrix and Wilfred entered the log cabin. It was very dark and smoky inside but nice and warm. They found a table near the fire and sat down. They ordered food and a bowl of water for Dog. It felt a bit strange in the inn. It seemed to have gone quiet as soon as they entered, like when the head teacher walks into a classroom and all the children stop talking. Slowly, the other customers started up their conversations again. In the corner there were two men who kept peering at a piece of paper and glancing over their shoulders at the new arrivals.

'Wilfred, Oi,' Beatrix said quietly. 'Is there something a bit odd about this place?'

Wilfred looked around. 'I don't think so. I mean, it is a bit strange that you have to eat with your hands and there are no knives or forks, but apart from that it seems pretty normal. Very busy, though.'

'I meant the other customers,' Beatrix said. 'They don't seem very friendly. I keep feeling like they're trying to – I don't know, *inspect* us.'

'I know what you mean,' Oi said. 'Just look at Dog. He's not happy.' Beatrix and Wilfred looked at Dog. He was sitting under the table. The hairs on his back were standing up and he was making a very low growling noise.

Beatrix pulled her toadstool hat lower over her head, so you could barely see her face at all. She stared through the low light, trying to see what the other customers looked like. The man staring at the piece of paper was tall, so tall his head almost touched the ceiling.

He stood very straight, like a soldier, but he was dressed like a farmer in a big red cloak. The man next to him also stood very straight. His hand kept reaching for something at his side.

Beatrix frowned. Who else did that? She recognised the movement. It was the same thing Uncle Ivan did whenever he was nervous or cross. He did it because he wanted to get his knife from his belt.

'*Oi*,' Beatrix whispered. 'I don't think those men are what they seem. Do you think you can get close enough to hear what they're saying without anyone noticing?'

'Course I can,' Oi said. Within a moment he'd ducked under the table and disappeared from view. He appeared again close to the tall man and crouched down, as if he'd lost something on the floor.

'How are your sheep doing in the snow?' he heard him say.

'Oh, you know, they're very sheepy. I keep losing them because they're all white and very hard to see. How are your cows?' the other man replied.

'Bit chilly. But at least the milk is nice and cold.'

'And how are your, er, your other animals, the ones with the tails?'

'The horses?'

'No.'

'The donkeys?'

'No, the, what do you call them... parrots?'

'Parrots? I don't have any parrots.'

'You know, the ones that lay the eggs.'

'Chickens? The chickens are fine.'

'Good good. I suppose all that fur helps keep them warm.'

'You mean feathers.'

'Yeah. That's it. The fluffy stuff.'

6

Wilfred's Amazing Magic Trick

Oi crept back to Beatrix's table.

'Those guys are definitely not farmers,' he said. 'Or if they are, they are the worst ones ever to exist.'

'How can you be sure?' Wilfred replied.

'Because one of them doesn't know the difference between a parrot and a chicken,' Oi said.

'How ridiculous,' Wilfred said. 'Everybody knows that chickens lay eggs. Parrots, on the other hand...' He paused.

'Parrots also lay eggs,' Beatrix said.

'Do they? I don't believe it. If they did we'd eat parrot eggs. Why don't we eat parrot eggs?' Wilfred said.

'Because the yoke is green,' Oi replied. 'My brothers told me. Anyway, there are only two parrots in the whole kingdom.'

'*Enough about parrots!*' Beatrix said in a fierce whisper. 'The real question is, why are those men disguised as farmers? If you ask me they look a lot like soldiers. They're standing very straight. Maybe they're Evil Army spies on their way to the palace. Maybe they –'

Beatrix stopped suddenly. The tall man was standing over their table, his bulky form blocking out all the light, just like a thunder cloud.

Close up, with his big red cape and long beard, he looked a bit like Father Christmas. An *Evil* Father Christmas. The other man stood behind him, so that Beatrix, Oi and Wilfred couldn't get up and go without pushing past him.

'Hello, travellers, good morning to you,' said the Evil Father Christmas in a loud voice that didn't sound at all like it was used to saying friendly things, like *Ho ho ho*. In fact, it sounded a lot more like it was used to shouting *KILL KILL KILL!*

'Hello,' said Oi.

'Hello,' said Beatrix.

'Good afternoon,' said Wilfred.

'Grrr,' said Dog.

The Evil Father Christmas pulled up a stool and sat at their table. He made a funny creaking sound as he sat down, as if his joints were made of metal.

He's either a soldier wearing armour under his farmer clothes, or he's a robot from the future sent back in time to change history, Beatrix thought. Why would a future robot disguise themselves as a farmer and visit a squashed-meatball inn in the middle of winter? If you could time travel, wouldn't you choose summer, and maybe a café by a nice warm beach?

Dog got up and sniffed suspiciously at the man's boots. Then he got hold of his long cloak with his teeth and pulled at it. Oi yanked him away quickly.

'Tell me, where are you heading to in this terrible weather?' Evil Father Christmas said.

Wilfred had gone a very strange pale-grey colour, as if he was half turned to stone.

'We, er, I, er, well, we're, er um…' he stuttered.

'We're a family of travelling magicians. We like to visit all the villages at this time of year, cheer everyone up a bit with some magic,' Beatrix said. 'My father's very cold, that's why he can't speak yet. He'll warm up soon. He's a brilliant magician.'

'Hmmm,' said the Evil Father Christmas.

'I suppose you'll be able to show us a few magic tricks then.' He folded his arms and looked at Wilfred in a challenging sort of way.

'Yes yes – of course,' Wilfred said quickly, blowing into his hands to warm them. 'What kind of trick would you like? I've got all sorts of tricks – the only one I won't perform is a flying spell. They never work.'

'Surprise me,' the Evil Father Christmas said. He sounded as if he would be very hard to surprise.

'Yeah, and surprise me too,' the other soldier added.

'Very well, do either of you have a knife?'

The Evil Father Christmas handed Wilfred a dagger with a skull and cross bones on it. It looked like a very dangerous weapon, not the kind of thing a farmer would have. Wilfred picked it up and examined it in the low light.

'Now, I need a saucepan from the kitchen,' he said. A few moments later a waiter placed a saucepan on the table. 'Excellent. Are you ready? I hope you're watching closely. I place the saucepan over the knife, tap it three times. Say the magic spell, and…' Wilfred lifted the saucepan. The knife was gone. Jeff the pigeon was underneath instead. The Evil Father Christmas stared at Jeff, who was looking even more confused than usual.

'That's great – but could I have my knife back please?'

'I'm afraid I've turned it into a pigeon,' Wilfred replied.

'OK. Thanks. But I've already had lunch, so I don't want a pigeon.'

'Why don't I order you a bottle of beer instead?' Wilfred said.

The man looked puzzled.

'I don't think that's –'

'A bottle of beer is much safer than a knife,' Wilfred interrupted, clapping his hands. A waiter appeared with brown beery liquid in a bottle. Wilfred took the bottle and poured the beer into a mug. Then he held up the empty bottle and shook it.

Inside, rattling against the glass, was the man's dagger. There was no way of getting it out without breaking the glass, and certainly no way of getting it in.

The two men couldn't believe their eyes. They both examined the bottle; they held it up to the light; they slapped each other on the back; they rattled it against the glass.

'If you'd like to see any more tricks, I can get another one from my cart outside,' Wilfred said. 'Norman and Harry, I'll need your help.'

Beatrix and Oi stared at Wilfred for a moment.

'Of course!' Beatrix said, in a deep voice. 'Come along, Norman.'

'You're so bossy, Harry.'

'That's because I'm a boy, boys are bossy. You should know that, Norman. Don't forget Jeff.'

They got up, taking Jeff and Dog with them. The two men were still examining the bottle, shaking the knife so it rattled against the glass.

'Quick, into the cart,' Wilfred said as soon as they were outside. He brushed off the fresh snow. 'We need to get away as fast as we can.'

Beatrix and Oi climbed in while Wilfred attached the reins to Jeff's bridle. They drove off along the track as fast as the horse could go, slipping and sliding on the frozen ground.

'They're looking for you,' Wilfred said, once they were a good distance away.

'*The Evil Army never gives up*,' Beatrix said. 'That was written on the dagger, wasn't it?'

She shivered, and it wasn't because of the cold. 'But thanks to your brilliant trick they were completely convinced that we were a family of magicians. How did you do it?' Beatrix said. 'That trick was impossible! It looked like real magic!'

Wilfred smiled and held onto the reins.

'I can't reveal all my secrets. Let's just say it involved an awful lot of planning. We've got a long way to go. Why don't you see if you can work it out? If you haven't figured it out by the time we get to Beluga, I'll tell you myself.'

7

Martin the Murderous Mulls over a Magic Trick

Oi and Beatrix weren't the only two people trying to work out how Wilfred had done the trick. Inside the inn, the large farmer who looked a bit like an Evil Father Christmas was still staring at the glass bottle. His name was Martin, Martin the Murderous. Martin loved two things. Being murderous, and magic. Because he worked as chief spy in General Burpintime's Evil Army, he had never told anyone about his love of magic, but he occasionally practised a few tricks when he was alone.

'Hey, Colin,' he said to the other spy. 'Where did that magician go? I thought he was going to come back with some more tricks.'

'So did I,' Colin said.

'Let's find him,' Martin said, heading outside into the cart park.

'They've gone. Must've been in a hurry,' Colin said, when they got there.

'Hmmmmmmm,' said Martin. It was a noise he made often – and those who knew him knew it meant he thought something wasn't quite right. Those who didn't know him thought he had something wrong with his tummy.

'Let's take a closer look at this bottle,' Martin said, holding it up to the light. 'There's only one way he could have got the knife in – that's by taking off the bottom of the bottle, filling it up with beer, then putting the bottom back on it.'

Colin grunted. Although he was also a spy in the Evil Army, he was more of a hide-in-the-dark-

and-whack-someone-on-the-head kind of spy. He didn't go in much for thinking and planning.

'Well he couldn't have done that, we'd have seen. So I suppose it was…' He couldn't think how the magician had done the trick. 'Actual magic?' he said at last.

'Of course it wasn't *actual* magic,' Martin replied. 'What I meant was, he couldn't have done all that while he was sitting there. It's not possible. So how did he do it?'

Colin scratched his head, which was beginning to hurt with all the thinking. 'Er… he travelled back in time, put the knife in the bottle, then went forward in time again?' Martin the Murderous gave Colin a look that made him feel like a squashed caterpillar.

'If he couldn't have done it here, he must have already had the knife in the bottle before he got here. Which means he already had a knife, which I think is a little strange. It's not as if soldiers from the

Evil Army go around handing out their knives, is it?'

Colin shook his head. 'Definitely not. I've got mine right here.' He felt his belt. 'I mean here,' he said, feeling his pocket. 'Oh, that's right – it's hidden in my shoe.' He pulled it out of his shoe, smiling.

Meanwhile, Martin was bending down and examining the ground.

'Come on, Colin. The snow's falling so fast it'll be hard to follow their tracks.'

'Maybe we should just stay in the nice warm inn instead,' Colin said. 'Have some more beer, see what's on the dessert menu.'

Martin shook his head. 'I don't think so. There's something not quite right about them. I want to ask the magician where he got that knife. And they left here very quickly, which is a little bit strange. Did you get a good look at them?'

Colin frowned. 'No, come to mention it. I was too busy watching the magician perform the trick.'

'So was I,' Martin said thoughtfully, 'so was I.' He took out the picture of Beatrix and looked at it once more. He couldn't remember exactly what the magician's assistants looked like.

'Get your things,' Martin said. 'We're going to follow their tracks, but we'll stay back for now. I don't want them getting suspicious.'

8

Riddletown

For the next day and night, Beatrix, Oi and Wilfred battled through snow, high winds and mists that descended suddenly and stopped you seeing more than two metres in front of you. Jeff the horse was covered in icicles. Jeff the pigeon was covered in icicles. Dog the dog was covered in icicles. Oi, Wilfred and Beatrix felt as if their bones had been taken out of their bodies, stuck in a freezer for a couple of hours, then slipped back in.

They were cold on the inside, which is one of the worst places to feel cold, because it feels as if you will never be warm again. They wrapped themselves in blankets and furs at night and in the morning they had to scrape ice off the wheels of the cart with frozen fingers, just to get it moving.

Once or twice they thought they could hear voices behind them, but the snow was falling so heavily it made everything muffled and strange.

'How long till we g-g-g-get there?' Oi asked.

'Th-th-th-th-th-thirteen days,' Beatrix replied through lips that were half frozen.

'Why have we st-st-st-st-stopped?' Wilfred said.

'D-d-d-d-d-d-don't know,' Beatrix and Oi said.

Beatrix rubbed her eyes with her frozen hands. They couldn't go any further – the road was blocked by two tall wooden gates. The gates were in the middle of a high stone wall that seemed to reach up all the way to the grey clouds.

'How strange,' Wilfred said, as he pulled the map from his pocket with shaking hands. 'The wall and gates definitely aren't on the map,' he went on. 'All it shows is the smudgy mark that looks like a snake that's eaten a Christmas tree. And, of course, General Burpintime's castle, which is in the mountains somewhere over there.' He pointed into the distance.

Beatrix climbed down from the cart. There was a sign covered in snow next to the gates. She brushed the snow off. 'It says *WELCOME TO RIDDLETOWN – no entry without a riddle.'*

'Riddletown?' Oi said. 'Sounds like a jolly place.

Maybe there'll be somewhere warm we can stay the night and a bakery selling bread and cakes.'

'I hope so,' Wilfred said, 'because there's another blizzard on the way.' The snow had started to fall again, covering them so quickly and so thickly that they might as well have been three snowmen.

'WHO GOES THERE?' shouted a not very friendly voice from on high. Beatrix stared up through the snow. She could see a guard in a tower, looking down on them.

'A family of magicians, just passing through,' she called out.

'You can only enter if you answer a riddle,' the gatekeeper replied.

'I wonder if everyone has to answer a riddle,' Beatrix said quietly to Oi and Wilfred. 'What if they needed a doctor or something, and it was an emergency?'

'Are you ready?' the gatekeeper shouted.

'YES!' all three bellowed back.

'Right, here we go. This is your riddle. *A-hem.*' The gatekeeper cleared his throat. '*I am found before Tony, as cold as can be, hard to make and even harder to see.*'

Wilfred, Oi and Beatrix stared at one another.

'Found before Tony?' Oi said. 'Who's Tony? What's he talking about? Sounds like nonsense.'

Beatrix brushed away the snowflakes from her face. *Found before Tony*, she said to herself. She didn't know any Tonys but there was an Antony who worked in the palace kitchen. Looking down, she saw that there was a log beside the gate. The snowflakes that landed on it reminded her of something.

Beatrix smiled. 'I think I've got it,' she said. 'What's Tony short for?'

'Well, Antony I suppose,' Wilfred replied.

'OK, and what comes before the Tony bit?'

'Ant?' Oi suggested, looking confused.

'Exactly. Now think, what ant is hard to make and even harder to see *and* as cold as can be?' Beatrix said, watching Oi as his eyes slowly lit up.

'Snow ants!' Oi shouted. 'Snow ants, that's the answer! They're hard to make and they're tiny!'

The large gates creaked open very slowly. They entered Riddletown, and the gates swung shut with a boom behind them.

9

The Riddletown Dragon

Beatrix, Oi and Wilfred stood on the main street in Riddletown. The houses were packed tightly together with tiny windows and big, heavy doors that looked like they were made to keep people out, not let them in. Grey smoke silently slipped out of grey chimneys and a river full of icy grey water flowed through the centre of the town.

'It's very grey here, isn't it?' Beatrix said. 'All in all, it looks like a big smudge of a town, as

if someone has drawn a picture, got cross with it, and then tried to rub it out. Maybe the smudgy snake mark on the map was actually someone trying to draw this place. If so, it's not actually a bad drawing.'

'What are all these funny-looking posters on the walls?' Oi said, looking round. The walls of some of the houses had posters stuck to them, which were soggy and peeling apart.

'Is it an advert for a circus or something like that?' Wilfred said, having a closer look.

'A circus that has a... dragon?' Beatrix said, looking at a blurry green shape with wings, a tail and a wicked grin. 'At least I think it's a dragon. And is that a small child next to it?' She paused, thinking for a moment, then said: 'Wait a minute, so that funny-looking snake on the map was meant to be a dragon?'

'Could be, it was a pretty poor drawing. There's writing on the poster too,' Wilfred said, trying to read the blurred words. '*Be good or be gone!* I must say this place does feel a bit creepy. Let's just find somewhere to stay the night, then be on our way.'

'I hope this town isn't obsessed with a made-up

dragon the way everyone back home was obsessed with Wobblers,' Beatrix said.

They got down from the cart and walked up the main street, crossing the bridge over the River Riddle. The water was black and icy.

'Looks like it's market day,' Beatrix said, 'so we should be able to get some supplies.'

There were stalls selling all sorts of things, from pots and pans to fresh eggs to sprout soup to books about riddles. There were animals too – chickens, sheep and cows in pens, huddled together against the cold – and lots of children helping their parents with chores.

'I say, I'm awfully sorry, but this bag of grain is very heavy. Would you mind terribly moving slightly to one side?' came a polite voice from behind Beatrix.

She turned to see a small child carrying an enormous sack on his back.

'Of course not. Can I give you a hand?' Beatrix said.

'No thanks. Quite all right. Thanks ever so.' The little boy swept past them, sliding along the icy street. With the big bag of grain on his back and his little legs hurrying along, he looked like a giant beetle.

'All the children seem *very* well-behaved,' Beatrix said. 'They must have come straight out of school and decided to help their parents at the market.'

'I was thinking the same thing,' said Oi. 'There's no mud on their clothes either. It's very strange. It's almost like they prefer working to playing. Personally, I prefer to have a little mud on my clothes – makes me feel at home.'

The square had a town hall with a clock tower on one side, and on the other side was an inn with wagons and horses tied up outside it.

'Oh, look over there, a cake stall! Let's get something to eat. I'm starving,' Wilfred said.

They walked over to the cake stall, where Beatrix's eye was caught by the local speciality, a riddle cake. It looked exceptionally delicious.

'What's that one made from?' Beatrix asked the girl behind the stall.

The girl was about eight years old and was smartly dressed with neatly combed hair. Her eyes were large and brown and, although she was smiling politely, Beatrix thought she looked a bit sad.

'I could tell you what it's made from, but I'd have to ask you a riddle. I'm afraid those are the rules of Riddletown, even for visitors.' She pointed at a sign behind her that said *No Riddle – No Service*.

'Why?' Beatrix said.

'Why what?'

'Why do you have to answer a riddle to buy a cake or enter the town?'

'You have to answer a riddle for everything here. It started hundreds of years ago when we were worried about strangers, before we had the walls and the gates. It was like a sort of code – the people of Riddletown knew the answers straight away. The strangers had to try to work it out.'

'But you've got walls and gates now,' Beatrix said.

'I know, but the riddles stayed. We have competitions each year to see who can come up with the best one. People take it very seriously.'

'What does the winner get?' Oi said.

'A badger hat –'

'A what?' Oi interrupted. 'A badger hat? That's even more strange than asking riddles all the time.'

'A badge, a hat and a special medal,' the girl continued.

'Oh right. I thought you said… never mind. So what's our riddle? We're very hungry!'

She frowned. 'I'll make it an easy one then. *What scary creature has never been seen, looks a bit like a goblin but is twice as mean?*'

Beatrix, Oi and Wilfred looked at one another. '**Wobblers!**' they all said together. 'Now let's buy some cake,' Wilfred added.

'Of course,' the girl replied, taking Wilfred's money and cutting the cake into slices.

'What's your name?' Beatrix asked.

'Matilda,' the girl replied.

'Nice to meet you. I'm…' Beatrix paused, 'Harry.'

'Harry?' Matilda replied, looking puzzled. 'Isn't that a boy's name?'

'Harry *is* a boy's name,' Beatrix said, realising she hadn't been talking in her deep voice. Or wearing a fake beard. 'But *Harriet* is a girl's name, and Harry is short for Harriet. Anyway, this is

Norman, and this is Bob,' Beatrix said, pointing at Oi and Wilfred.

'We're a family of magicians,' Wilfred said. 'Just passing through, performing tricks to cheer people up.'

'Well if you need anywhere to stay in Riddletown, my mother and father have an inn. It's just over there.' Matilda pointed at a house with a thatched roof on the other side of the square. 'Normally you have to answer two riddles to get a room but there's a special offer at the moment. Half price – one riddle per room.'

'Great, more riddles,' Oi said under his breath.

Beatrix was wondering what kind of a place this was. Riddles for rooms and dragons on the walls. It all felt *very* strange. She hoped the snow would stop falling so they could be on their way first thing in the morning.

10

Be Good or Be Gone!

Beatrix, Oi and Wilfred walked across the market square with Matilda to the inn. It was a large building with a thatched roof and white-washed walls that bulged outwards, like a soggy loaf of bread. Matilda led them to a big room at the top of a rickety staircase.

'You can come down for dinner as soon as you're ready,' Matilda said. 'It's sprout soup.'

'Um, what else have you got?' asked Oi.

'Sprout pie.'

'I'm not sharing a room with Wilfred after he's eaten sprout soup and sprout pie.' Oi looked truly horrified.

'Maybe we'll just have some bread and cheese and a bit more cake instead,' Beatrix said. 'By the way, what are all these posters for? We saw a few of them in town.' Beatrix was pointing at a poster on the wall. This time, you could actually see the picture clearly, and it was even more creepy than the faded posters they'd seen earlier. It showed a strange green dragon holding a naughty-looking child's hand. The child's clothes were all muddy and he had a catapult in his pocket, some cake stuck to his face and a bag of sweets in his other hand. Nearby was a broken window.

You couldn't help feeling a bit sorry for him, even though he did look very cheeky. The poster had the same words printed on it:

Be good or be gone!

Matilda glanced nervously over her shoulder at the open door. She crossed the room and closed it.

'*No one talks about the posters,*' she whispered.

'But we all try to be good, very good, because otherwise...' She stopped. There was a knock at the door and a kind-looking lady appeared. She had red cheeks as if she'd been working in a hot kitchen and an apron tied round her very large waist.

'Hello, Mum,' said Matilda.

'You're needed downstairs, my dear,' she said to Matilda. 'Some farmers have just arrived in town and want to have dinner. Funny-looking farmers they are too – they stand very straight and look very stiff.'

Beatrix looked at Wilfred in alarm. *The soldiers were in their hotel?*

Matilda's mum turned to Wilfred. 'How are you settling in? Like the room?'

'It's very nice thanks,' Wilfred said in a nervous voice.

'Excellent. Well, make yourselves at home and I'll bring you some supper.'

As soon as she'd gone, Wilfred turned to Beatrix and Oi:

'They're here!' he said. 'The soldiers are downstairs! I think we should leave.'

Beatrix frowned. 'We can't,' she said. 'It'll look suspicious if we rush out now. Who leaves an inn just before bedtime? And besides, we can't get very far in this weather. We're stuck in this town. We'll stay out of their way. If they're the same ones we saw before, then hopefully they already believe we're a family of travelling magicians. Anyway,' Beatrix looked at the poster on the wall, 'I want to know what's going on. There's something not right about this place. Did you see how sad Matilda looked when we asked her about the poster? There's something she's not telling us…'

11

Beatrix Goes for a Swim

Beatrix couldn't sleep. The straw bed was itchy and uncomfortable. Wilfred was snoring like an elephant with an orange stuck up its trunk and Oi kept talking in his sleep about different kinds of mud. Jeff the pigeon was flapping about in his cage and Dog was making the kind of whiffy pongs only dogs (and occasionally dads) can make.

Beatrix twisted and turned. She wanted to

leave Riddletown as soon as possible but she also wanted to find out what was going on. *Time for some answers*, she said to herself, getting up. She was going to find Matilda.

Beatrix crept downstairs, to see that the two farmers – also known as Martin the Murderous and Colin – were still eating and drinking by the fire. She kept as close to the wall as possible so the floorboards wouldn't creak, holding her breath with each step.

Matilda was in the kitchen, washing up wooden plates and pots and pans in a big barrel full of soapy water. She looked as if she might fall asleep and go headfirst into the barrel at any second.

'I can't believe you're still up!' Beatrix said.

Matilda jumped in surprise, then smiled when she saw who it was. 'There's not much left to do – I should be able to get an hour or two's sleep before morning.' Beside her was a huge pile of dirty dishes. It looked like it would take *forever* to finish.

'Do you have to do this every night?' Beatrix asked.

'Yes, but it's not usually this busy,' Matilda replied. 'And I used to have my brother Jack to help me.'

'Why doesn't he help any more?' Beatrix said.

'He's gone – he wasn't good.' Matilda looked around before lowering her voice. 'Just like they say in the posters,' she whispered, '*Be good or be gone!* I think he was taken.'

'Taken by what? You're not suggesting it was a dragon, are you?' asked Beatrix.

Matilda shrugged. 'I don't know. He's not the only naughty child who's disappeared. Lots of others have too.'

Beatrix frowned. 'Well that explains why all the children we saw today were so well-behaved.

Why don't their parents look for them?' she said.

'They've tried. My mother and father asked in all the nearby villages and explored every inch of Wobbler Woods, but no one's ever actually seen a child disappear. My mother says she's seen something that looked like a dragon, but she only saw its shadow. It was sneaking about in the backstreets and then it simply disappeared. That's why there are signs all over town, to warn us. One day your brother or sister or friend is here, the next day they aren't.'

BOOM BOOM BOOM!

Someone was banging on the kitchen door, someone with a very heavy fist. A fist that was more used to bashing people on the head than knocking on doors.

'I'll see who it is,' Matilda said. 'The farmers might want some more food or drink.' Before Beatrix could stop her Matilda ran across the kitchen to open the door. Beatrix looked round

for a hiding place. There was
nowhere to hide – nowhere
except the large barrel full
of greasy water with bits of
sprout floating in it. Beatrix
held her nose and swung over

the top of the barrel into the water.

Matilda opened the door.

'Just you in here, is it?' said a gruff voice.

Matilda looked round, and saw the bubbles in
the washing-up barrel.

'Oh yes. Of course. It's just me,' she replied,
looking up at the very tall man standing in the
doorway. He was all twitchy and cross-looking,
as if he'd put too much chilli sauce on his chips.
His beard bristled out from his cross face like the
spines on a hedgehog's back. He was about as big
as a medium-sized grisly bear standing on its hind
legs. Martin the Murderous.

He looked round the kitchen with his twitchy

eyes and rubbed his twitchy beard with the back of his enormous hammer-hand.

'Just me in here. That's all,' Matilda repeated nervously. 'Absolutely no one else.' The man stopped looking round the room and stared at her.

'Funny, I thought I could hear voices. Have a look at this,' he said, unrolling a piece of paper. 'Do you know this girl?' the man said.

'Er, nope. I can honestly say I've never seen anyone who looks quite like that,' Matilda replied.

'Well, I need to search every room in your inn. I have to find her.'

'That would be pointless,' Matilda said. 'You and your friend are the only guests at the inn.'

'Huh,' Martin said, peering over the top of her head.

'Time for you to go,' Matilda said. 'And if you bang on any more doors I'll have you thrown out. You'll be sleeping in the snow. Goodnight.'

Martin the Murderous cast one more look

around the room, made a *Hmmmmmm*-type noise and walked away. Matilda closed the door, and as she did so a very bedraggled Beatrix pulled herself out of the barrel, gasping for breath.

'I thought he'd never go!' she said. 'Thanks ever so much for getting rid of him. That was very brave.'

'Not at all. Here, take this.' Matilda threw a

cloth at her. 'Are you the girl in the picture? It was a pretty funny-looking drawing, but there was something familiar about it. Why is that farmer trying to find you?'

'He's not a farmer – he's a spy from the Evil Army. They want to kidnap me. They think I'm going to destroy them all and take over their land because of a curse. Ridiculous, isn't it?'

'Hang on. You mean *you're* Beatrix the Bold?' said Matilda. 'The queen with magic powers who'll one day lead an army of Wobblers to

 defeat the Evil Army in a mighty battle? That's one of my favourite stories, but I thought it was just made up! I didn't realise there was an *actual* Queen Beatrix. I certainly didn't ever think she'd end up in my washing-up barrel in the middle of the night.'

Beatrix shrugged. 'Neither did I. And to be honest,

I don't really believe in all that stuff. What I want to do is see my parents in the Kingdom of Beluga – that's where I'm going. I haven't seen them since I was tiny…' Beatrix stopped. She suddenly felt very sad. Sad and tired. And… angry. She thought of Matilda's poor little brother, Jack. The idea that children could be taken away and *never* see their parents again – well, she couldn't go on with her journey to see her own parents without getting to the bottom of this. It wouldn't be right.

'I'm going to help you find your brother, and the others. This can't be allowed to happen,' she said, rubbing her hair with the cloth. She had a feeling the smell of sprouts would stay with her for ever.

'Using your magic powers?' Matilda asked. 'That would be brilliant!'

'It's more likely we'll end up using funny disguises than magic powers,' Beatrix said. 'What do all the children who disappeared have in common?'

'They're all naughty.'

'And when were they taken?'

'When no one else was around.'

'So if we get you to be naughty all day, I mean *really* naughty – worse than your brother ever was – and then make it look like you're alone, maybe this dragon thing will appear and try and take you. We'll follow it and get you back, along with all the other children. What do you think?' Beatrix grinned.

Matilda frowned, then a little spark of light appeared in her eyes.

'I think I can manage that,' she said.

12

How to Catch a Dragon

Beatrix and Matilda hurried upstairs.

'Oi, Wilfred, wake up!' Beatrix said. 'We need your help.'

Oi sat up in bed.

'Are we there yet?' he said in a sleepy voice.

'We need a plan. Someone or something is taking the naughty children of Riddletown and they're never seen again. No one can find them.'

'Wait, what... you mean like in the posters?'

Oi rubbed his eyes. 'So we're not going to Beluga any more?'

'Of course we are. But before we do, we have to find out what's going on here. I can't carry on my journey to see my parents when all these children have disappeared.'

'But if we stay here and try and sort this out, we won't be able to cross the mountains before the spring thaw and the avalanches start,' Wilfred said. He got out of bed, wrapped himself in a blanket and put a couple of logs onto the fire to warm up the room.

'That's just a risk we'll have to take,' Beatrix replied.

'And, of course, the Evil Army spies are staying in this inn,' he added.

'I know, I know. But this is important. It was Matilda's mother who made those posters, to warn people. Matilda's brother Jack has gone. They think there's a dragon that takes the children.'

'Why does it only take the naughty ones?' Oi said.

'I don't know – maybe it thinks their parents won't care,' Beatrix said.

'Or maybe it wants to steal all that naughty energy and use it for something,' Wilfred said.

'We can get Matilda to be naughty, that's pretty easy,' Beatrix said. 'But what's really going to get that dragon's attention? Matilda, are there any stories about the so-called Riddletown Dragon? There must be some – people make up all sorts of stories about the things they're scared of. Like Wobblers – three eyes, fat bellies, all that stuff. What do they say about the Riddletown Dragon?'

Matilda frowned and thought for a moment. 'Some people say it lives in the woods and only eats raspberries and hummus.'

'Raspberries *and* hummus?' Oi said. 'Surely not together? What kind of an animal is it?!'

'Other people say that conkers are actually dragon poo.'

'Gross!' said Beatrix.

'And my teacher says the dragon hides in the tunnels under the mountains and only comes out on Wednesdays in a month that has two Os in it.'

Beatrix, Oi and Wilfred looked at each other, running through the months of the year in their heads.

'Isn't that just October?' Beatrix said eventually.

'And Joon,' Matilda replied. 'And Jooly. That's what my teacher says anyway.'

'I think your teacher might need a new dictionary,' Beatrix said.

'Maybe if we mix up a bowl of raspberry hummus we can get it out this month,' Oi said.

'I doubt it,' Beatrix said. 'All this really tells us is that you can't pay too much attention to what people say. The reason the Evil Army wants to kill me is because people say I'm going to take over their land with an army of Wobblers. And I don't have an army of Wobblers. Wobblers don't exist. I don't think dragons exist either. Hang on...' Beatrix smiled. She had an idea. If lightbulbs had been invented there would have been one shining above her head. They hadn't, so it was a candle instead.

'Why don't we make up our own dragon? Just like we did with Wobblers. What's going to get the attention of the Riddletown Dragon more than anything else? Another dragon!

Especially if this one is controlled by a naughty child.'

Matilda, Oi, Wilfred and Dog were silent, thinking it over.

'And some raspberry hummus?' Oi said at last.

The four of them (and Dog) crept downstairs. The spies had gone to bed. Oi and Wilfred carried oil lamps, but they didn't cast much light. They just made everything a little yellow and sickly-looking, like an old banana.

They hunted about amongst the old junk in the cellar, looking for anything a bit dragon shaped.

'What about this?' Beatrix said, picking up a broom. 'If you hold it upside down and drape a sheet over it it'll look like the neck and head of a dragon. Matilda could wave it about so it seems as if it's alive.'

'This will make a good tail,' Wilfred said, picking up a half-stuffed pillow.

'For the wings we could use these,' Matilda said, holding up a pair of dusty curtains.

'Have you got any conkers?' Oi said. 'We could always use those for the –'

'Right, Matilda,' Beatrix interrupted. 'You hold the broom. I'll put this sheet over the top. We'll tie an old scarf round its neck to give it a bit of shape and stitch on the wings and the tail. Do you have any green paint?' she asked. 'Otherwise you'll look more like a very tall ghost than a dragon.'

'Don't think so,' Matilda replied from under the white sheet, 'but there should be some paint in a pot by the door. Can you cut a hole so I can see?'

Beatrix carefully sliced through the material with her knife, making two eyeholes.

'Looks like you're going to be a red dragon!' Oi said, picking up the pot of paint and splashing red spots over the white sheet. 'Can we make it breathe fire?'

Beatrix held up a pair of bellows that were lying beside the fireplace. (Bellows were what they used in the olden days to blow more air into a fire, a bit like a pump for a lilo.)

'We might not have fire, but if we fill the bellows with paint, then Matilda can squirt it out of the dragon's mouth.'

'A paint-breathing dragon?' Matilda said.

'Exactly – the Paint-breathing Dragon of Riddletown. Look out everyone, you're about to get splatted!'

13

Everyone Gets Splatted

It was early morning, and Martin and Colin were sitting in the dining room of the inn, waiting for breakfast to appear. They called for Matilda every couple of minutes, but she didn't come. In the end, Martin went into the kitchen to try to find her. There was no one there, so he simply bellowed, '*BREAKFAAAAAAST!*' as loudly as he could.

A few moments later, Matilda's mother came down the stairs.

'Matilda should be here,' her mother said. 'I don't know where she's gone.'

'Can't you rustle something up for us?' Martin said. 'We don't need much – just bacon and eggs, bread and jam, a couple of fartinpants, maybe some porridge too.' He patted his stomach. 'And a jug of warm milk. All that farming is hungry work, looking after the parrots and things.'

'After the what?'

'Chickens,' Colin said. 'Not parrots.'

'I'll get right on it. Let me just check if the other guests want breakfast too.'

'The other guests?' Martin said. 'I didn't think anyone else was staying here.'

'Oh yes, there's a family of travelling magicians. I'll be back in a mo.' Matilda's mother disappeared upstairs.

'Family of travelling magicians!' Martin said excitedly. 'They're here!' He raced upstairs, with Colin following close behind him.

They waited in the corridor as Matilda's mother knocked on the door to Beatrix's room. No one answered. She knocked again, then she opened the door with one of her keys, peered inside, frowned, closed the door and locked it again.

'No one there?' Martin said.

'They've gone out. Must be early risers.'

'Must be. Wonder what's so important they need to get up this early? It's not as if they can go anywhere with all this snow...'

He stopped. There were voices outside, excited shouts from children and adults, dogs barking, chickens clucking. Even the cows seemed to be mooing a more excited moo than usual.

'What's all that commotion?' Matilda's mother said.

'We have it, it's here!' a voice called out.

'The Riddletown Dragon! Ladies and gentlemen, boys and girls, it's been captured at last. No more should you be afraid. Come and see its mighty, er, red spots. And its terrifying tail, which doesn't look at all like a half-stuffed pillow.'

Martin and Colin ran down the stairs and out the front door. They saw a very curious sight. It was the magician and boy from the squashed-meatball inn, leading what looked like a cross between a dragon and a pair of curtains across the market square. A rope was tied loosely around its neck and the dragon's head dipped up and down as if it was struggling to break free.

'It's them!' Martin said. 'The magician and his assistant. Well, one of his assistants. The girl's not there. What are they up to? Is this another trick? Are they going to make the curtain-dragon-thing disappear and reappear before our very eyes?'

'I'd be very surprised if they can make *that* fit into a bottle,' Colin said. Colin and Martin joined the crowd that had gathered in the town square, trying to look as farmer-like as possible, pushing their way to the front.

'Stand back, be careful. We used powerful magic to bring it under control,' Wilfred said.

'A magic raspberry,' Oi said. 'And a magic bowl of hummus.'

'Are you sure it's *the* Riddletown Dragon?' said one of the stall holders. 'It looks a little bit like a ghost that's swallowed a broom.'

'Then caught chicken pox,' another said.

'And it's February – it's not even Joon, or Jooly. Why's the dragon out already?'

'Of course we're sure it's the dragon,' Wilfred replied. 'And don't talk too loudly – you'll upset it. And when it gets upset, it breathes –'

'Fire?' said a voice in the crowd. The front row moved back.

'Not this one – no, this dragon's a different species,' Wilfred said. 'Scaly dragons breathe fire, red-spotted curtain dragons breathe…' He paused.

People were crowding round, trying to get a look at the dragon. Matilda was struggling underneath the sheet to hold onto the broom, it kept slipping out of her hands. It looked as if the dragon was shaking its head up and down. She gripped the broom handle under her arm and grabbed hold of the bellows, which were heavy and full of sticky red paint. She aimed them out of the mouth. It was hard to see what she was doing. It was hard to hear what was going on too, it just sounded like a lot of noise. She pushed the bellows together.

They made a wheezy, parping sound (very similar to a grandmother after Christmas dinner) and sprayed the thick red paint in a wide semi-circle.

A chorus of *angry* voices rose from the crowd.

Matilda wasn't sure if she'd got it all out, so she squeezed the bellows together again. She heard the splatter of paint once more. People were pulling at her costume now. She could hardly see anything through the eyeholes, but she waved the head about and ran forward, swinging the broom.

'*Ouch!*'

'*Oof!*'

'*Watch it!*'

She could see blurred shapes through the eyeholes. The dragon's head was banging into people. Matilda ran forward, straight into a stall selling eggs. They crashed to the ground, cracking and splattering all over the place. More voices cried out. She turned again, knocking over another stall with her tail. This one was selling sprout soup.

The greeny, mushy liquid poured out of a huge saucepan over the snowy ground, making the first ever sprout slushy. (Also the last ever sprout slushy.)

In the middle of the crowd a tall, thin man in a black cloak was watching all this with interest. It had been a while since he'd seen such naughtiness in Riddletown. And a very long time since he'd seen a red-spotted curtain dragon. In fact, he wasn't even sure he'd ever heard of such a thing. *A naughty child, no doubt*, he thought. He took out a notebook and wrote down what he saw, then he climbed onto his horse and galloped out of the town.

14

Peas and Marshmallows

General Burpintime was sitting at the head of
the table in the huge dining room in his
castle. A delicious lunch had been laid out and
he was wondering what to eat first. There was a
whole chicken, a whole pig, a whole salmon, a loaf
of bread in the shape of a hedgehog (his favourite
kind of bread) and a big bowl of peas. Peas were
the only vegetable he would eat, and he'd only
eat them if he could have one marshmallow after

each pea. It took him
a long time to eat a
bowl of peas, but the
more he ate, the more
marshmallows he could
have, so he usually ate them first.

He was tucking into his ninth pea and was
starting to feel a little full, when there was a knock
at the door.

'Come in!' he shouted. But the room was so
big that the messenger didn't hear.

'COME IN!' he shouted, even more loudly. The
door still didn't open, so he put the pea down, slid
out of his high chair and opened the door himself.

'Yes?' he said.

Outside stood the tall, thin man in the black
cloak. 'News from Riddletown. Just in. Another
naughty one,' he said, breathing heavily.

'Ooh lovely,' General Burpintime replied. 'It's
been a while.'

'Well, this one is quite something. I've never seen anything like it.' The messenger handed Burpintime a note, bowed his head and left the room.

Burpintime opened the note. He was about to read it when Esmerelda barged into the dining room. He hid the note behind his back.

'Lunch time is it? Why didn't you tell me? I'm starving. What are you having?' she said.

'Peas, mainly. I like to look after myself. They're very healthy. And filling. Help yourself.'

Esmerelda looked at the peas but didn't take any. Instead, she took a big slice of hedgehog bread, some chicken and half a side of salmon. She sat down next to Burpintime.

'What's that you're hiding in your hand?' she said, as she tucked into her lunch.

'Nothing. Nothing to do with you anyway.'

'Is it news about Beatrix? If so you should tell me. I need to know.' Esmerelda didn't trust General Burpintime. She thought that if he found out where Beatrix was, he'd simply capture her and not hand over the gold. That's the problem when baddies work together. There's no trust.

'No, it's not about Beatrix. It's just a report. A secret report. I'm a *very* important man around here and I like to know what's going on, especially in Riddletown. Now, if you'll excuse me, something urgent has come up. I need to get ready to go out.'

'Out where?' Esmerelda said. 'Surely you need to wait here for news of Beatrix?'

General Burpintime stared at her. No one told him what to do – except his boss, the Evil Overlord. Who did she think she was, asking him where he was going? As if it was any of her business!

'Out wherever I want. I have important things I need to do.' He glanced at the note he'd been given, holding it under the table so Esmerelda couldn't see, then set fire to it with one of the candles on the table. He blew it out quickly, stamping on it for good measure.

'Goodbye, Esmerelda. I shall return later tonight. Help yourself to the peas. Don't eat my marshmallows. I've counted them and I'll know.'

As soon as he was gone Esmerelda picked up the piece of paper from the floor. It was mostly burnt but she could still see some writing on it.

Child dressed as dragon — extreme misbehaviour.

Very strange, Esmerelda thought, helping herself to a marshmallow from the enormous bowl next to the tiny bowl of peas. What on earth was Burpintime up to?

15

Wilfred and Oi's Big Mistake

Wilfred and Oi had snuck away from the market and joined Beatrix in one of the small streets off the square while Matilda charged around causing mayhem.

'She's certainly got the hang of being naughty. If this doesn't make the Riddletown Dragon come out of hiding then I don't know what will,' Wilfred said, as Matilda swung the dragon's head down towards the ground, knocking a chicken high into the air. The poor bird landed in a ball of feathers in the sprout slushy, flapping its wings and shaking itself down, before bending over to taste the slushy. It shook its head and coughed in a chickeny sort of way and walked off.

'I haven't seen any sign of it yet. Matilda might need to wear the dragon outfit all day if it doesn't come soon,' Beatrix said.

'Even when she goes to school?' Oi asked.

'Especially at school,' said Beatrix. 'The teachers would hate it! I'll stay close to her in case the dragon turns up. Why don't you two go back to the inn, get some supplies then meet me by the school? If you could get a couple of fartinpants with bacon in the middle, like a sandwich, that would be great. And some cookies. Riddle cake if they have any left. Be careful though, I saw the two spies from the inn in the crowd watching the dragon.'

Oi and Wilfred slipped away, checking to see if the spies were in the market square.

'Can you see them?' Wilfred said.

'No,' Oi said, looking round. 'I can see a lot of mess – red paint splatted all over the place, a couple of very unhappy chickens and a sprout slushy – but I can't see any spies. Let's go.'

This was a mistake. Everyone makes mistakes, but some mistakes matter more than others. This one would matter quite a lot. You see, Martin the Murderous didn't get to be chief spy in General Burpintime's army by being a complete idiot. He knew a little bit about spying. He knew that the travelling magicians had left their cart outside the inn. And he'd seen that they had left their things in the bedroom when Matilda's mother opened the door. Adding these two facts together, he decided it was extremely likely that they would soon return to the inn.

So instead of waiting out in the cold, trying to chase them across the market square and down little alleyways, he was waiting at the inn with Colin.

'Come on, Colin, looks like our magical friends are on their way back,' Martin said, peering out of the window. 'Let's wait for them in their room. Give them a nice surprise.' He held up a key to show Colin.

'How did you get that?' Colin said.

'Easy. I took it off the innkeeper when she wasn't looking.'

Wilfred and Oi didn't realise what was about to happen, because Wilfred and Oi didn't know they'd made a mistake. But they would do soon. Wilfred took out his key and opened the door to their room at the inn.

'Well hello there,' Martin said in a very deep voice. Oi was surprised that the word *hello* could sound like a threat, but somehow it did. Martin reached out and took the key from Wilfred's hand.

'Why don't you two have a seat? My friend and I have got some questions for you.'

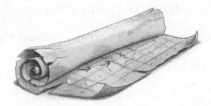

16

The Truth About Dragons

'**A**ny sign of the Riddletown Dragon?' Matilda said. She was standing with Beatrix, out of breath after running around causing mayhem and trying to escape the angry stall holders. The residents of Riddletown were tidying up the mess. The sprout soup stall was now selling sprout slushies and the egg stall was now selling scrambled eggs.

'I haven't seen the dragon yet, so I think you're going to have to stay in costume. How do you fancy going to school dressed as a red-spotted, paint-breathing curtain dragon?'

'I like it!' Matilda said, pushing the broom up and down so that the dragon nodded. 'It's actually quite good fun charging about the place and banging into things.'

Beatrix and Matilda made their way to Riddletown School, sneaking down narrow streets between the houses so that they stayed out of sight.

'Best of luck,' Beatrix said when they reached the school gates. 'Make sure you refuse to take off the costume, even when your teachers order you to remove it. I'll wait for you over there.' She pointed at a little street opposite the school. 'I'll be hiding behind that doorway.'

Beatrix wrapped her coat tight around her and pulled her toadstool hat down over her ears. She hoped Oi and Wilfred wouldn't take too long getting breakfast. Even though she was supposed to be keeping an eye out for the Riddletown Dragon, all she could think about was a bacon sandwich and a riddle cake.

Beatrix waited and waited but there was no sign of Oi and Wilfred and there was no sign of the dragon. She was so cold her teeth were chattering, her feet were numb and she felt as if she had frozen sausages for fingers. She wanted to go back to the inn to find her friends but she couldn't in case the dragon snuck into the school and took Matilda.

The minutes turned into hours and Beatrix had to jog on the spot to try to stay warm. The people of Riddletown lit torches along the main street and in the town square as it grew dark. By now she was convinced Oi and Wilfred were in trouble, but there was nothing she could do about it. She had to wait by the school for Matilda.

The flaming torches hung in metal cages from the buildings and gave off a very jumpy, nervous sort of light. It made the shadows come to life.

The school gates opened at four o'clock and the children came out. Well, the children and a very naughty, red-spotted curtain dragon. A teacher was waving her hand at Matilda, telling her off and shooing her away. Beatrix couldn't hear what the teacher was saying but it looked as if her face was experiencing a series of mini explosions. The dragon kept shaking its head and the other children were laughing.

'How did that go?' Beatrix said, as Matilda approached the doorway she was hiding in.

'Good fun! These bellows are pretty good for spraying school lunch as well as paint,' Matilda said.

'You didn't!' Beatrix replied.

'*I* didn't. The dragon did! Although I did then have to spend most of the afternoon outside the head teacher's office. And they've taken away my playtime for the next ten years because I refused to take off the outfit, so please tell me you've seen the dragon lurking about somewhere.'

'Not yet. And I'm worried about Oi and Wilfred – I haven't seen them all day. Let's go back to the inn. You go ahead – we'll give this dragon one last chance to appear.'

Matilda set off down one of the many tiny lanes that ran between the thatched houses. The town was like a maze. If you weren't on the main street or in the market square there were no lights and you could get lost very easily. Beatrix waited till Matilda was a short distance away, then slipped out of the shadows and followed her.

The ground was icy underfoot and the night smelt of smoke and dinners being cooked. Sometimes when Beatrix passed a hut or a house she could hear voices from inside and they floated on the air, free of their bodies. She knew it was only people talking, but she was thinking about the dragon, and thinking about the dragon made everything seem strange and a little bit scary. Dragons weren't real. She *knew* this. But it was a lot easier to tell herself that during the day than at night when she was following a friend down dark little streets in a strange town where children vanished.

Matilda had stopped and was standing very still in the middle of the street. Beatrix pressed herself into the doorway of one of the houses.

'Hello, is anyone there?' she heard Matilda call out.

Silence. Then a sort of rustling noise, like a sparrow or a mouse moving through dead leaves.

'Who are you – what do you want?' Matilda said, taking a step backwards. Beatrix moved forward; she could feel her heart thumping against her chest.

'What do I want? Why, I heard there was another dragon in town, so I wanted to see it,' a quiet voice said. There was something very familiar about the high-pitched tone.

'Yes, but you do know I'm not a real dragon?' Matilda said. 'I mean, real dragons don't have curtains for wings and a pillow for a tail. Are you real?'

'Of course I am.'

'Then how come you can talk human?'

'I taught myself.'

'How?'

'Er…' The dragon hesitated. 'With words of course. You just put them together, one in front of the other. Like walking. Little babies learn to talk, and all they can do is poop and sleep – it's really not hard. Not for a clever dragon like me.'

'Is that what you do when you're not talking?' Matilda said. 'Poop and sleep?'

Beatrix covered her mouth and tried not to laugh.

'No! Not all the time. No more than usual.'

'How often is usual for a dragon? Three conkers a day?' Matilda said.

'None of your business! And that thing about conkers is not true. Conkers are conkers, not dragon poo. And before you ask, I hate hummus, quite like raspberries and it doesn't matter how many Os there are in the month. I come into town whenever I feel like it.'

'And you felt like it today?'

'Why yes, of course. I wanted to meet you, I wanted to meet the child that so loves dragons she's decided to dress up as one and charge around the market square like you just don't –'

'Care?'

'Exactly.'

Beatrix moved forward, careful not to make a sound. She wanted to get a closer look at the dragon. It was smaller than she thought it would be. It had a very fat belly. She could make out its

wings and a tail which dragged along the ground. Its skin looked very old and saggy, like an ancient elephant.

The dragon took a couple of steps towards Matilda. It moved like a chicken, and it had tiny arms like a T-rex. Beatrix could now see it was carrying two large brown sacks.

'Anyway,' the dragon said, 'I would like some help. I'm on my way to a party and these bags of cakes and sweets are very heavy. If you help me carry them, I'll give you an enormous party bag full of sweets and chocolates for you to take home. And you could stay for the party too. You're already dressed up.'

Matilda was feeling less nervous now. The dragon was more weird than scary.

'You're a dragon on your way to a party?'

'Yes. What's so strange about that?'

'Nothing really, it's just that when you think of dragons, parties aren't the first thing that comes to mind. Breathing fire, tick. Terrorising villages, tick. Kidnapping children, also tick. But parties… they don't feature in many stories with dragons.'

'Well I happen to like parties!' the dragon said, his voice getting even more high pitched. 'What's wrong with a dragon that likes parties?'

'Nothing at all,' said Matilda. 'Where's this party of yours?'

'Oh it's not far. Follow me. It's no distance at all.'

The dragon moved faster than Beatrix expected, hurrying down the street. Matilda kept up with it, walking quickly and carrying one of the sacks. Beatrix followed close behind. Where on earth were they going? The only way out of Riddletown was through the enormous gates.

The dark streets grew narrower and narrower, until there was hardly any street left between the houses.

'It's this way,' the dragon said, 'I can almost hear

the party music. We're nearly there.' He turned down an alley. Matilda couldn't hear any music. Nor could Beatrix, as she waited in the shadows. The dragon ran forward a few steps then waited by a door.

'You are so kind,' he said to Matilda. 'So very kind, I don't know what I would have done without you. Come this way, through the door, and you can have your sweets. Lots of sweets, lots and lots of sweets!'

Matilda approached the door. The dragon knocked three times. The door opened. Matilda and the dragon disappeared inside. Beatrix ran towards them, afraid of losing Matilda. As she approached she saw something that made her shiver in terror – a cage, a big metal cage, big enough for a child. It was hanging above the door! The door slammed shut and she heard the cage fall to the ground with a great thump.

Beatrix ran to the door and tried to open it. It was locked. No, no, no! This was no good, no good at all. If she couldn't follow Matilda then it was all for nothing. Not only would she have failed to rescue Matilda's brother, she'd have failed Matilda too!

She shoved the door with her shoulder. It wouldn't budge. She ran round the side of the house to see if there was a way in from the back, but a high stone wall blocked her path. She tried to climb, jumping up, trying to get a grip with her fingers, but the stones were flat and smooth and there was nothing to hold on to. She needed help. She needed Wilfred and Oi.

17

Beatrix's Amazing Magic Trick

Beatrix ran back through the streets as fast as she could, making sure she remembered each twist and turn in the maze of passageways. One left turn, two to the right, one to the left. It didn't take long, and soon she was back on the main street, running towards the inn.

She skidded on the ice outside, banging into Matilda's mother who was busy cleaning snow off the path.

'Woah! Hello there!' she said.
'Have you seen Matilda? She's
usually home by now.'

Beatrix didn't know what to say.
She couldn't exactly tell Matilda's mother she'd
just seen her daughter get taken by the dragon.

'She'll be home soon. I promise. Are my friends
here?'

'Oh yes, they're upstairs. They've been there all
day. Talking to the farmers.'

'Wait… which farmers?' Beatrix said. 'The ones
who farm sheep or the ones who farm parrots?'

'The ones who farm parrots. Are you OK, my
dear? You suddenly look awfully pale.'

Beatrix stood very still. First Matilda had been
taken, now Wilfred and Oi were trapped with Evil
Army spies. How could she get them out of there?
Beatrix ran over to the cart and climbed onto
it. She opened up the chest with shaking fingers.
Time for a disguise. And a magic trick.

A few moments later, Beatrix was standing outside the door to their room in the inn, one hand raised, ready to knock. She took a deep breath. She was no longer Beatrix the Bold. She was Fernando the Fantastic. She had a pillow stuffed under her top, a fake beard and a wizardy hat pulled low over her head. Around her shoulders she wore a cape and she'd even attached Oi's fake nose. She knocked on the door and waited.

'Who is it?' came a deep voice from inside.

'I am Fernando the Fantastic, and I have a delivery for Bob the Magician, a box of magic tricks, amazing magic tricks, all the way from… far away. The other side of the world.'

Martin the Murderous scratched his head. He and Colin had been waiting all day for the girl to come back, and the longer he spent with 'Norman' and 'Bob', the more suspicious he became that they were not who they said they were. And no matter how many times he asked, Bob wouldn't tell him where he got the Evil Army knife he'd used in his bottle trick.

In fact, he was now so suspicious and so fed up with the silly answers he was getting (especially from Norman) that he'd tied them both up, stuffed socks in their mouths and locked them in a cupboard.

'Leave the magic tricks outside the door – I'll pick them up later,' Martin said.

'Oh no, I can't do that. These tricks are far too expensive. Someone might steal them,' Beatrix replied.

'Come on then,' said Martin, opening the door. 'But be quick, we're waiting for someone.'

Beatrix bounded into the room.

'I am Fernando the Fantastic,' she announced, putting the box of tricks down on the floor and looking round the room. 'Where's Bob? I need to show him how to do the new trick he ordered. It's very complicated.'

Colin and Martin looked at one another, then Colin said: 'Bob has just popped out with Norman. Show us instead and we'll tell him.'

Beatrix thought she could hear a strange thumping sound coming from the wardrobe.

'Very well,' she said, opening the box. She took out the chains and padlock. 'What's that noise?'

'What noise?' Martin replied. 'I don't hear anything.'

'Neither do I,' said Colin.

'That banging sound, coming from the wardrobe,' Beatrix said.

'Oh that,' Martin replied. 'It's just rats. Horrible, stinky rats. There are lots of 'em running about the place.'

'Horrible, stinky rats,' Colin repeated, with a smirk on his face.

Beatrix looked at the wardrobe.

'I see,' she said. 'Rats can be a nuisance. Especially ones that get caught easily and have to be rescued,' she said, a little more loudly. 'Anyway, the trick. Here's how you do it. Pay close attention so you can tell Bob.' She lifted the chains out of the box. 'First I wrap these chains all around me, like so...' she said, rapidly winding the chains about her waist. 'Then I fasten the chains with a padlock. Help me, would you?'

Martin fastened the padlock in place. He was really rather intrigued to see how the strange little man with the high voice and the big nose would get out of this.

'Now, if we had a lake, I would throw myself in

it and escape under water. But we don't, so instead I will escape from these chains before your very eyes!' Beatrix turned her back on Martin and Colin. She felt with her fingers for the special button that would release the lock. Then she threw off the chains with a terrific, 'Ta-dah!'

'Not bad,' Martin said. 'Did you keep the key to the padlock hidden in the palm of your hand?'

'Oh no, it's quite simple. Let me show you.' She grabbed the chains and ran them round Martin and Colin as quickly as she could, making sure she looped them around their wrists and ankles.

'First you make sure the chains are nice and tight, then you fasten the lock,' she said, clicking the padlock in place, 'then…'

'Then what?' Martin said, thinking that the chains were rather tight around his tummy and wrists. 'And why's your beard falling off?'

'Then you open the cupboard,' Beatrix said, ignoring Martin, 'untie your friends… and ruuuuuunnnn!'

As Beatrix opened the cupboard, Oi and Wilfred tumbled out. Beatrix untied them and the three of them darted down the stairs and out the front door, slipping and sliding on the icy street.

'Come with me, fast as you can,' Beatrix said. 'We have to find Matilda. Into the cart – I'll show you the way.'

They jumped onto the cart, with Beatrix sitting in the driving seat. She flicked the reins.

'Come on, Jeff, let's go!'

Jeff the pigeon started flapping about in his cage.

'Not you, Jeff, the other Jeff.'

The other Jeff looked over his shoulder, gave a horsey shrug, shook off the snow then began a slippery gallop towards the house Matilda had disappeared into.

18

The Vanishing Footprints

They raced through the streets with Jeff's hooves thumping the fresh snow. The house Matilda had disappeared into was silent and dark.

'Doesn't look like there's anyone here now,' Oi said.

'Well this is where they took her,' Beatrix said. 'Let's climb over the back wall and see if we can sneak in.'

They scrambled over the high stone wall, using ropes from their cart.

'Have you got candles?' Beatrix whispered when they were on the other side.

'Yes, in my pocket,' Oi said. A strange barking sound came from his coat.

'Barking candles?' Beatrix said.

Jeff the pigeon made a cooing sound.

'And cooing candles?'

'I thought they might both come in handy. Dog can smell the soldiers before we see them and we might need to send Uncle Ivan a message with Jeff.'

Wilfred used a fire stone and a piece of metal to make a spark and light a piece of dry wool, blowing into it so the flames caught. Oi held the candlewicks in the flame, and passed a lighted candle to Beatrix.

'Are you *sure* you saw a dragon?' Oi said.

'I saw something that looked like a dragon,' Beatrix replied, looking for the back door. 'Or an enormous chicken. Here, the door!'

She tried the latch. It was unlocked. She opened it carefully, making sure she didn't make a sound. The house was cold and damp and silent.

'There's no one here,' she said.

'What a strange house,' Wilfred whispered, peering round the room. It wasn't like a normal house. There was no furniture, no chairs or tables or bed. The house was just one big room, all the way to the roof. On one wall was a fireplace, but that was it. It was clear there was no one inside.

'Are you sure Matilda and the dragon came in here?' asked Wilfred.

'Of course I'm sure. There was a cage just inside the door. The dragon must have carried her away in it – we're too late.'

'Unless...' Wilfred said.

'Unless what?' Oi replied.

'This house isn't what it seems. Their boots will have been wet with snow and mud

when they came in from the street, but I can only see footprints in one direction on the floor.' He held a candle close to the floor. Beatrix knelt down next to him.

'Look,' Beatrix said, 'they go to the fireplace. Then they stop.'

Dog was standing by the fireplace, sniffing at it and pawing at the stone. He was giving out a low growl, the kind of growl he usually only used when there was danger nearby. Or when he needed to go to the toilet. Oi hoped he didn't need to go to the toilet.

Beatrix gave her candle to Wilfred.

'Hold this – I want to check something.' She felt her way around the fireplace. In the palace where she'd grown up there were secret passageways all over the place. She had a feeling she might be able to find one here too. The stone fireplace had funny-looking faces carved into the top of it. They were meant to look jolly and smiling but there was something sinister about them – it was almost as if they were laughing at her. She pulled at them and tried to twist them, but they didn't move. Then there were two stone dogs, one either side of the fire. She pushed the one on the right. It didn't move. Then she pushed the one on the left. This one did move, but only a tiny bit.

'Wilfred, Oi, give me a hand,' she said. Oi and Wilfred rushed to her side. They pushed and pulled at the stone dog, with the real Dog jumping up at it and yapping.

'It's no use,' Wilfred said. 'It's solid – we'll never get it to move.'

He was wrong. All of a sudden, the dog's head sprang back and the whole fireplace swung outwards with a scraping sound, knocking the three of them over like skittles.

Behind it was a great black hole of darkness.

'A secret passage,' Wilfred said, getting to his feet and peering behind it.

'What are you waiting for? Let's go!' Beatrix said, pushing past him.

19

The Tunnel under the Mountain

Beatrix went first, holding the candle in front of her. Oi and Wilfred and Dog followed. They were standing in a very cold and very dark room. Without any warning, the fireplace door slammed shut behind them. It made a huge thud that shook the building.

'That doesn't sound good,' Oi said.

Beatrix held her candle close to the wall, trying to see if there was any way they could open the door again from this side. She couldn't find one. Wilfred felt along the wall with his hands, looking for some kind of lever or switch.

There was nothing.

'I suppose the only way we can go is forward,' she said. 'It has to lead somewhere.'

Steep stone steps led downwards and the air got colder and colder as they descended. On the walls were *strange* paintings. Children holding hands,

walking along a pathway. Some of them looked like they were eating sweets. The air was damp and some of the paint was peeling off the walls, so a few of the children's faces were blank and empty. One of them was missing an eye, but still smiling a strange, half smile.

It made Beatrix think of all the children who had disappeared, all the ones who'd been led away by the dragon. She felt sad and angry, but more than that, she felt determined to find out what had happened to them.

'Where do you think this passage goes?' Oi said.

'We'll find out soon enough,' Beatrix replied. She hoped Matilda and the dragon weren't too far in front of them. They'd had quite a head start. Dog was running beside her. She checked her candle. It had already burnt down halfway.

The floor of the tunnel was paved with smooth, flat stones. The ceiling was low, and Wilfred had to stoop so that he didn't hit his head. He kept

whistling and humming songs
to himself.

They walked and they
walked but still they didn't
get to the end of the tunnel.
Beatrix lit another candle. It felt like the
passageway was going upwards now.

'We must have reached the edge of Riddletown,'
she said. 'I wonder what's above our heads?'

The walls were no longer smooth but rocky
and jagged. Water dripped and there were puddles
on the ground.

'I think we're going through the mountain,
behind Riddletown. It feels more like a cave than
a tunnel.' Beatrix stopped in her tracks.

'Isn't General Burpintime's castle in the
mountain above Riddletown?' Beatrix asked,
remembering the map. Wilfred, Oi and Dog also
stopped.

'It is,' Wilfred replied.

'And if we keep heading upwards, my guess is we'll end up…' Beatrix didn't finish her sentence. She wasn't sure she wanted to.

'We'll end up with Burpintime chopping us into little pieces?' Oi said.

'I wasn't going to say that,' Beatrix said, 'but now you mention it, I do think we should be a little more careful. I don't want to lose any pieces of myself. Apart from maybe my hair – it's a little long at the moment. He could chop off some of my hair.'

'I don't think that's what Burpintime will chop off,' Wilfred said. 'If he wanted to give you a haircut he'd just chop off your head. You'd have no hair, but you'd also have no head.'

'Well I don't want that – so, from now on, only speak if absolutely necessary, and only as a whisper.' Beatrix was going as fast as she could over the uneven ground. Oi, Wilfred and Dog were close behind. It felt like the tunnel went on for ever. It was like having to do a school cross-country run. In the dark. With the possibility of ending up in a castle filled with soldiers who want to kill you when you get to the end.

'Come on, Dog,' Beatrix said, turning round. 'You run ahead. Give us a little growl if there's anything unusual.' Dog scampered off, wagging his tail. Even though he was quite an old dog, he was still pretty fast and sure-footed on the rocky ground.

Beatrix, Oi and Wilfred followed him. Up and up they went, further into the mountain. Sometimes the tunnel opened out into huge caves, and their footsteps echoed and multiplied so it sounded like there were twenty of them. Sometimes it narrowed till it was so small they could only just squeeze through. It felt less like they were running through a tunnel, and more like they were running through the insides of some strange, giant monster.

At last, after what seemed like an eternity (an eternity being the length of two maths lessons and a wet playtime added together), the path became smooth and flat again. They were all out of breath and took a moment to rest. Dog was ahead of them and they couldn't see what he was looking at, but he was standing still. His hackles were raised and he was giving off a low growl.

'Shhh,' Oi said. 'Good boy, come here.' Dog turned and ran back to Oi, but he wouldn't stop growling. 'Stop making that noise – you sound like Wilfred,' Oi said.

Beatrix crept forward. What was making Dog growl? The air in this part of the tunnel was different. It was fresher, colder, not as damp. Dog's nose was twitching. She walked forward. They'd reached the end of the tunnel. It opened onto a moonlit valley. On the opposite side Beatrix could see General Burpintime's castle, perched like an eagle's nest in the rocks. Next to it was a tall waterfall that poured into a wide river that ran along the valley floor. The river flowed fast, churning the silvery-black water.

Next to the river, Beatrix could see what looked like a small village. Even though it was the middle of the night, they could see figures moving about. Flaming torches marked out paths, and in the middle of the houses a huge pit glowed red with the embers of an enormous fire.

It looked like a fiery red stamp on the ground.

'Let's get a closer look,' Beatrix said.

'Matilda must be down there somewhere.'

She skidded down the hillside, with Oi and Wilfred following.

Now that they were closer, they could see that the tiny dots hurrying about were children. Some were pushing wheelbarrows, others were moving large boxes. They were dressed in rags. Soldiers from the Evil Army shouted at them whenever they slowed down.

Beatrix could see a cauldron suspended on chains over the fire pit. Next to the fire pit was a barn. She couldn't see what was going on inside, but behind the barn was a conveyor belt. This reached up the mountain, and disappeared into a cave just below Burpintime's castle.

Two children had to run in a hamster wheel to make it move, and other children were loading boxes onto it.

'What is this place?' Oi said. 'Do

you think this is where General Burpintime makes the weapons for the Evil Army?'

'I'm not sure,' Beatrix said, staring down at the bottom of the valley. 'It could be. The soldiers guarding the children are definitely from the Evil Army, but I can't see what they're making. Hang on, isn't that Matilda down there?'

Beatrix pointed at a small girl. A soldier was walking behind her. She was carrying a heavy-looking wooden box and every time she slowed down he poked her with a stick.

'Let's see if we can get a message to Matilda using Jeff,' Beatrix said.

'We left Jeff in Riddletown,' Oi replied.

'Jeff the pigeon,' Beatrix replied, scribbling a note onto a piece of paper, 'not Jeff the horse. Unless you've got a flying horse hidden in your pocket.'

Oi took Jeff carefully out of his pocket and Beatrix tied the note to his leg.

'OK, Jeff,' she said. 'Let's see if you can get the message to Matilda.'

'What does it say?' Wilfred asked.

'It says, *Help is on its way,*' Beatrix said.

'Oh good,' replied Wilfred. 'I was beginning to worry. When will it be here?'

'It's *us*. We're the help!' Beatrix replied. She lifted up her hands, opening her palms so Jeff could fly away. Jeff looked confused, but then Jeff always looked confused, on account of his cross-eyes. He turned to Beatrix, made a cooing sound, then flapped his wings and flew into the night sky.

'Where's he gone?' asked Wilfred.

'No idea,' Beatrix replied.

20

A Very Short Chapter
(with a very long title) in which
Martin the Murderous Draws a beard
on Beatrix the Bold

'There must be a way to unlock this padlock,' Martin said, as he shifted and wriggled and tried to shake off the chains. It was no good, they were wrapped tightly around him and Colin.

'Maybe Fernando used real magic to open it,' Colin said. 'Maybe that's how he escaped.'

'There was no Fernando,' Martin replied irritably. 'It was a girl, the same girl who was with Bob and Norman at the inn with the squashed meatballs. She just had a fake beard. And a fake belly. Now, if I could get my hands on that padlock...' His thick fingers felt their way along the chain, then wrapped around the lock. It was awkward trying to examine the lock, especially with the chains digging into his arms. He felt something, pressed it. The lock clicked open.

'Ha!' he said. 'I knew it. Classic spring-loaded release system.' He managed to work the lock free. The chains rattled onto the floor and he stood up and stretched his massive arms, shaking out the stiffness.

'Now, where's that picture?' he said. Colin pulled off his chains and reached into his pocket.

'Here you are,' he said, unrolling it and placing it on the table. Martin held a candle next to it and examined it closely.

'Pass me a piece of charcoal from the fire, would you?' he said. Colin passed him a piece of charcoal. Martin drew a beard onto the face with

the charcoal, then added a
hat and a bigger nose.

'What do you think?'
he said. 'Fernando the
Fantastic looks an awful lot like
Beatrix the Bold, wouldn't you say?'

Colin frowned. 'I suppose he does. I wonder if
they're related.'

Martin stared at him. Sometimes he couldn't
understand how Colin had got a job as a spy.

'Go and tell General Burpintime we've found
her, fast as you can. I'm going to try and follow
their tracks.'

21

Vice President of Spying and Extreme Danger

Colin's horse skidded to a halt outside General Burpintime's castle. He climbed down and ran past the guards without even stopping to insult them. (This was how Evil Army soldiers usually greeted each other – with a couple of well-chosen insults.) He ran across the drawbridge, through the courtyard, up the spiral staircase and barged through the large wooden doors into the dining room. Of all the places to find General Burpintime, he was most likely to be in the dining room. Breakfast, lunch and dinner weren't so much three meals as one long continuous meal.

'We've found her!' Colin said, gasping for breath as he tumbled into the room. 'Beatrix the Bold. Seen her with my own eyes I did.'

General Burpintime was sitting at the table with Esmerelda the Terrible. As usual, they were in the middle of an argument. This time about where he'd been all afternoon and why he still hadn't found Beatrix.

'You've found her, where?' Esmerelda asked quickly.

'Yes, where did you find her?' General Burpintime said. He hated the way Esmerelda always acted as if she was the boss, asking questions first, helping herself to the best food.

'In Riddletown, at the inn. She tried to disguise herself as Fernando the Fantastic but I saw through it. You don't get past Colin just because you've got a beard and pillow stuffed under your top. Martin wanted you to know straightaway, so here I am.' Colin performed a funny little bow then stood very straight. He wondered if General Burpintime would give him a medal now or whether he'd just shake his hand and offer him a promotion. Maybe to Vice President of Spying and Extreme Danger.

General Burpintime didn't do either of those things. Instead he said:

'Well don't delay, bring her in. I want to see this girl; I want to see the one who is supposed to lead an army of Wobblers and destroy our lands. I want to see the person who's going to make the curse come true. Especially as it now obviously *won't* come true.'

General Burpintime rubbed his hands together. The day was getting even better. It looked like his spies had actually done what they were supposed to do. And he really was curious to see the girl. It would be like meeting a character from a story or a legend, someone who was supposed to have special powers and everything. Well, she didn't seem so special now. He couldn't understand why his boss, the Evil Overlord, was so worried about her.

'A-hem,' Esmerelda said, making a coughing sound. Nobody paid her any attention.

'A-HEM!' she said again, this time more loudly.

Burpintime turned to her. 'What's the matter with you? Got a cough or something?'

'My gold,' Esmerelda said. 'I want my gold. This was thanks to me. You couldn't have done it without me. We had a deal.'

'Your gold? Oh yes, of course I remember your gold. Don't worry. You'll get what you deserve.' Burpintime looked at Esmerelda. He didn't need to give her anything at all. It wasn't like she had an army. He could feel an evil laugh coming on, a deep *Woo-ha-ha-ha-ha*, so he stuffed a marshmallow into his mouth to try and stop it. Then he stuffed another in because the first one tasted so good.

'Come on, where is she?' he said to Colin, through a mouthful of marshmallows. 'Bring her in, I want to see her.'

'Ah, well,' Colin said, taking a step backwards. 'When I say we *found* her, I don't mean we *captured* her.'

'Wait – what?' Burpintime said. Little specks of sticky white marshmallow splattered over the soldier, as if a seagull had just flown overhead. 'Are you saying she escaped?'

'Not exactly,' Colin said. Although that was sort of what he was saying. 'We know where she is – she's in Riddletown. Martin the Murderous is on her trail and you know how expert he is at catching people.'

'So Martin's captured her, has he?' Burpintime said. 'He's got her locked up in a little cage and everything?'

'Er, maybe. By now, maybe, she's in a cage. I mean, probably that will definitely have happened by now. If not, then, er, Martin will still be trying to find her.'

General Burpintime made a *Nnngggghhhh* sort of noise, picked up a bowl of peas from the table and flung them across the room. Colin ducked. The bowl crashed into the door and the peas rolled over the floor.

'I'm going to Riddletown,' Burpintime shouted. 'I want to make sure Martin doesn't mess this up. Beatrix has already escaped from us once before.'

'I'm coming too – you need my help,' Esmerelda said. 'Frankly I've been extremely disappointed by both the quality of your spies and your soldiers.'

Burpintime picked up another bowl. He was about to throw it at Esmerelda when he realised it was full of marshmallows. He put it down on the table, took out the marshmallows very carefully, one by one, then threw it at her.

Esmerelda ducked and it crashed into the wall.

'Colin, get the horses ready,' Burpintime said, 'and at least twenty soldiers. We leave at once,' he went on, then paused to eat a marshmallow. And another. And another.

'Well, what are you waiting for?!' he shouted, before eating another marshmallow.

22

The Worst Soup in the World
(and that's including sprout soup.
And sprout slushy,
which is a sort of soup)

Wilfred, Oi, Beatrix and Dog watched the
children working. It was as if they were all
moving to the beat of the same drum. If they'd
once been naughty, then that naughtiness had
been well and truly drained out of them by the
hard work the Evil Army soldiers made them do.
(A bit like when you get to the end of a popsicle
and all the fruity sweetness is gone and you're just
left with icy water.)

'If we're going to get out of this alive with all those children, we need a plan,' Wilfred said.

They couldn't go back down the tunnel, and the valley had high cliffs on one side and a raging river on the other.

'I have a plan. A very rough plan,' Beatrix said. She cleared her throat. 'Stage one, we rescue the children so they can see their parents again; stage two, we escape. Stage three, we carry on our journey to Beluga and I get to see my parents. Because I'd really like to see them soon. Got that?'

Wilfred scratched his chin thoughtfully. Oi scratched his bottom, also thoughtfully.

'How will we rescue them?' Oi said.

'How will we escape?' Wilfred added.

Beatrix stared at the factory.

'As Uncle Ivan taught me, if you want to win in a battle, you have to understand your enemy. You have to know the battleground. You have to give yourself the advantage.' She paused.

 'You two wait here. I'm going to see what's going on down there. I'll be back soon.'

'Wait a minute, you can't just...' Wilfred began. But Beatrix was already running down the hill.

'I'll go with her,' Oi said, racing after Beatrix.

'OK, fine — I'll just stay here with Dog,' Wilfred muttered to himself.

Beatrix and Oi hid in the snow, watching the children work. They counted fifteen guards. It was hard to tell how many children there were, because they kept disappearing into the mine, the big barn and the low stone building next to it, but she thought there were at least twenty.

Now they were closer, they could see that the giant cauldron that hung over the fire was actually more like a saucepan. Whatever was inside it was boiling and bubbling and spitting, like a pool of hot lava. Two boys stood on a platform next to it. They looked exhausted. Beatrix thought one of them looked a lot like Matilda.

'Do you think that's Matilda's brother, Jack?' she said to Oi.

'Could be. Whatever are they doing?' Oi replied. Buckets filled with a strange gloopy mixture were lined up on the platform. The two boys kept looking over into the bubbling mixture, as if they were waiting to see when it was ready, then they poured the gloopy stuff from the buckets into the huge saucepan.

'*What on earth is going on?*' Beatrix whispered. It seemed more like they were making a disgusting dinner than weapons for General Burpintime. A thin young girl in a torn yellow dress carried another two buckets from the stone building next to the barn and passed them to the boys on the platform.

'Thanks, Anna, be careful,' said the one who looked like Jack.

'*No talking!*' growled the guard standing near the fire pit.

'Let's find out what they're doing in there,' Beatrix said. They crept towards the low stone building Anna had come out of. What they saw took their breath away, quite literally – the smell was so bad they could hardly breathe. It smelt of boiled bones and bits of animals and all sorts of disgustingness. It was *even worse* than sprout soup. Or a sprout slushy. There was another cauldron over a fire. This one was a lot smaller, but still big enough to fit at least three medium-sized children in it.

Beatrix and Oi ducked down in the shadows and watched as a small boy scooped a strange jelly off the top of the stinky soup. He ladled it into buckets so that the girl in the ragged yellow dress could carry it up onto the platform for the two boys to tip into the saucepan.

'I can't see Matilda,' Beatrix said, staring into the smoky room.

'Let's try the barn,' Oi replied. They crept forward, crouching low. There were two guards standing next to the enormous fire pit to keep warm. One was busy eating a cheese and onion sandwich and the other one was busy telling him how much he hated the smell of cheese and onion sandwiches. They both had very strange haircuts – they were completely bald on top with long hair at the sides, as if someone had glued their helmets on for a joke, then pulled them off, taking all the hair with them.

Beatrix and Oi slipped past them. They stood outside the barn. Beatrix peered into the entrance. Only children were inside – no guards. They ducked through the doorway and hid in the shadows behind a stack of wooden boxes.

It was a large room, lit by flickering candles. In the centre was what looked like a huge white mattress. Above it hung an enormous and very sharp-looking blade. Three children pulled the rope to lift the blade, then they let it go. It whooshed down onto the mattress, slicing it in two. They pulled the rope so that it lifted the blade again, whilst two other children moved the big fluffy white mattress so that it could be sliced into smaller pieces.

'What is this place?' Oi said.

Behind her, Beatrix heard the rattle of chains. She turned to see what was going on. The giant saucepan that was over the fire was spinning upside down. A big white fluffy thing fell out and was caught by the children on a large wooden plate below. They carried it into the barn.

Beatrix and Oi watched the children raise the blade once more. There was no mistaking what was underneath now.

They let go of the blade.

'*Marshmallow!*' Beatrix whispered. '*They're making and slicing marshmallow.*'

The stinky stuff they poured into the saucepan was a jelly made from bones. They mixed that up with the boiling sugar to make the marshmallow. (I know this is hard to believe, but that *really is* how you make jelly, and jelly plus boiling sugar equals marshmallow.)

Once the marshmallow was cut into smaller pieces, children packed it into wooden boxes, ready to put on the conveyor belt so it could be carried up the mountain to Burpintime's castle.

'Look, there's Matilda!' Beatrix said.

In a corner of the room, a very tired-looking Matilda was helping to move the boxes of marshmallow. Beatrix and Oi ran towards her, staying close to the wall. The enormous blade made a whooshing sound as it cut another huge marshmallow mattress in two.

'Matilda – *psst*. It's me,' Beatrix said.

Matilda jumped, then turned towards Beatrix. Her face was a mixture of relief and fear. 'Thank goodness! I thought I'd lost you once the dragon took me into the house in Riddletown. Where have you been?'

'Trying to find you – oh, and rescuing Wilfred and Oi from the Evil Army spies. What happened to the dragon?'

'It disappeared once we arrived here. There are mines under the mountain, it might hide out in there. The soldiers tell us that they'll feed us to the dragon if we're bad.'

'So it was real then? A real dragon? A real dragon, with a funny high-pitched voice?' Beatrix asked, her voice full of doubt.

'I don't know, it was dark. And I've never seen a real dragon. The other children say it sometimes walks through the factory at night, checking the marshmallows.'

'I bet it does. Everyone loves a marshmallow,' said Oi.

'I think we saw your brother Jack,' said Beatrix.

'At least, we saw a boy who looked a lot like you by the enormous saucepan just outside.'

'Yes, that's him! It's one of the most dangerous jobs here – if you fall into the boiling sugar then...' Matilda shook her head. 'That's just like Jack, he's not scared of anything. We've got to get everyone out of here, but how? There are cliffs and a river blocking our way, not to mention all those guards. Can you use your special powers to make us all disappear, send us back to Riddletown?'

'I don't have any special powers and I certainly can't make all the children disappear, but...' Beatrix peered through the barn door at the huge saucepan hanging over the fire. 'I might be able to make the guards disappear, if I can get them all in one place. And I think I might have an idea for how we can get away.' She pointed at the huge mattresses of marshmallow that were stacked in the corner of the room, ready for slicing. 'Marshmallow floats in hot chocolate, doesn't it?'

'Of course.'

'So it will definitely float on the river. And that river must be the River Riddle, which flows all the way to Riddletown. Are you any good with boats?'

'Don't know. I've never been in one,' Matilda replied.

'Neither have I. Doesn't matter. All we have to do is hold on and try not to eat the boat. How many children are here?'

'About twenty. There were more, but Jack told me some children managed to climb up the cliffs and escape,' she said. 'I don't know where they went – they didn't come back to Riddletown.'

'How strange,' Beatrix said. 'Now, we'll have to make sure we get away as quickly as possible. You stay here. We'll go and get Wilfred. We have to work fast.'

23

General Burpintime Gets Mad

General Burpintime, Colin, twenty soldiers and Esmerelda raced to Riddletown on the fastest horses in his army, clattering over the cobbled roads.

'Who goes there?' the guard at the Riddletown gates shouted as they approached.

'General Burpintime. I command you to open these gates immediately.'

'Can't do that, I'm afraid. You'll need to answer a riddle first.'

'ME?' Burpintime shouted. 'ME?! Didn't you hear my name?! I'm General Burpintime! I don't answer riddles. Here's a riddle for you instead – *if you don't open the gates immediately, what cake do you think you'll end up looking like?*'

'Er, hmmm…' The gatekeeper wasn't sure if this was an actual riddle, or just one of those questions people asked but didn't really expect an answer to, like when teachers say, *Why can't you just be quiet?*

'A pancake!' Burpintime exploded. 'That's the cake you'll look like. Because I'll flatten you – I'll have them roll barrels full of rocks over you till you're flat as a pancake. Then I'll squeeze lemon juice and sugar on you and feed you to my soldiers for breakfast. Now open the gates before I send my soldiers up to drag you down!'

The gatekeeper looked down.

'All right, all right,' he said. 'I'll open the gate.' Honestly, when he got the job as gatekeeper they hadn't told him it would be like this. *Ask a riddle, open the gate, close the gate, snooze. Ask a riddle, open the gate, close the gate, snooze.* That's all they said he'd have to do. There was no mention of marshmallow-chewing generals threatening to make him into a pancake.

General Burpintime charged through the empty streets towards the market square. The soldiers and Esmerelda raced behind him, trying to keep up.

His horse skidded to a halt outside the inn.

Martin was pacing up and down nervously. Burpintime jumped off his horse and grabbed Martin with both hands.

'Where is Beatrix – have you got her?' he said.

'What... who... er – no, Sir General Sir.' It took Martin a few moments to realise who he was talking to. He wasn't expecting General

Burpintime to come to Riddletown in the middle of the night. He'd assumed that once he got the message he'd just pop a few marshmallows in his mouth, rub his hands together,  sit down in his high chair like a big baby and wait patiently by a nice warm fire. (Everyone knew that this was Burpintime's favourite way to spend an evening. And a morning. And an afternoon.)

'I haven't captured them, but I have tracked them – they took their cart through the town then left it outside a house not far away. Trouble is, they seem to have vanished into thin air. Not that I believe that's possible,' he added hastily. 'I'll show you.'

General Burpintime stared at the cart. What was Queen Beatrix doing here, by the house that hid the entrance to the secret passage through the mountains? She was supposed to be on her way to see her parents in Beluga. This definitely wasn't the way to Beluga.

He didn't like it. He didn't like it at all. He turned to Esmerelda.

'This girl, this Beatrix, she's up to something. She isn't on her way to Beluga to see her parents. She's gone into the house. And the only thing in this house...' he said.

'Yes?' said Esmerelda.

Burpintime frowned. He didn't like telling Esmerelda his secrets.

'*In this house,*' he whispered, '*is a secret passage through the mountains to my marshmallow factory.*'

Esmerelda raised her eyebrows. A marshmallow factory, and a secret passage? The general really was full of surprises. There was silence for a moment. Then Esmerelda said, 'Maybe Beatrix wants to steal your marshmallows. She can be very annoying like that – she stole ten rooms in my palace from me. I only had a hundred or so left.' Then she took a marshmallow out of her pocket and popped it in her mouth.

General Burpintime turned towards her, his face the colour of boiled beetroot. He made a strange noise, a noise Esmerelda had never heard before, at least not from a human. A screamy, screechy wail of a sound. If you squished the word 'No!' with a rolling pin and stretched it out like playdough, you'd be halfway there.

Anyone in Riddletown who was sleeping was now fully awake.

'Follow me,' General Burpintime said, pulling himself together and unlocking the door to the house. 'I want all my soldiers to surround the marshmallow factory. And I've got a little surprise of my own that I might unleash upon Queen

Beatrix – a terrifying surprise, something so terrifying it will terrify anyone who sees it so much that they are well and truly...'

'Terrified?' Esmerelda said.

'Exactly,' General Burpintime said. This time he did let out an evil laugh. A terrifyingly *evil* laugh. So terrifying he scared himself a little bit, almost did a wee, and had to stop laughing.

24

The Great Escape

Beatrix and Oi crept out of the barn and ran back to Wilfred.

'Where've you been? I've been waiting ages,' Wilfred said in a fierce whisper. 'I thought something had happened to you!'

'We've found Matilda and her brother. And you'll never guess what they're making – it's marshmallows! This place is a giant marshmallow factory!'

Wilfred stared down at the factory. He looked a little bit impressed, and a little bit horrified.

'Wow – I mean, I like marshmallows, but that's taking it to a whole new level,' he said.

'I've worked out a way to rescue everyone and escape. But the first thing we have to do is make the guards disappear,' Beatrix said.

Wilfred frowned. 'I hope you're not expecting me to do some sort of magic trick, because I'm telling you now, I can't fit all those guards up my sleeve. And even if I could, they'd probably chop my arm off.'

'No, you don't have to do a magic trick. Come with me.'

Oi, Wilfred and Beatrix made their way through the snow, crouching low. There were guards everywhere and they didn't have long before sunrise. Even though they'd been up all night they weren't feeling tired – they were fizzing with nervous energy.

'See that barn?' Beatrix whispered to Oi and Wilfred. 'That's where they take those huge pieces of marshmallow. Follow me.'

The two guards who'd been arguing about a cheese and onion sandwich were still arguing about a cheese and onion sandwich. They didn't see Beatrix, Oi and Wilfred as they ducked into the barn.

The children who were slicing marshmallow and putting it into boxes stopped what they were doing and stared at them.

'It's OK,' Matilda said, running forward to greet Beatrix. 'They're here to help us.'

Beatrix turned towards them.

'My name is Queen Beatrix the Bold. You might have heard of me from those stories they tell around the campfire. Or if you've read *Beatrix the Bold and the Curse of the Wobblers*. Or maybe you haven't heard of me at all. Doesn't matter. I'm here to rescue you.'

'Well, technically you're here because you were on the way to Beluga to find your parents,' Oi said.

'All right, all right. Technically that's why I'm here. I was on my way there when I met Matilda and she told me about her brother and all the missing children. I couldn't carry on my journey to see my parents knowing you might not see yours again. And I hate the fact that everyone is so scared of that dragon. I don't even think it's a *real* dragon. Now, here's what's going to happen, and I'm going to need all your help.'

For the soldiers who were guarding the children it had been a very dull night. Nothing had happened. The same as last night, and the night before, and the night before that. And it had been ages since any of the children tried to run away.

Sometimes they wished one of them would, just to give them something to do.

The guard who had been eating a cheese and onion sandwich had finished eating it, but the guard who'd been complaining about the smell of the cheese and onion sandwich had not stopped complaining.

'How would you like it if I stood here all night eating peanut-butter sandwiches?'

'I wouldn't care.'

'You would if you were allergic to peanuts.'

'Well I'm not. So I don't care. And you're not allergic to cheese and onion sandwiches.'

'I might be. Maybe that's why I can't stand the smell. It's my brain warning me to stay away…' He paused. He was distracted by what looked like a small child, jumping up and down on the conveyor belt.

'What's going on up there? Is that what I think it is?'

The other guard followed his gaze.

'It looks as if… it looks as if one of the children is dancing. Wait a minute, what's that in his hand? Is it a –'

'Marshmallow?'

The two guards were so stunned by this, that for a moment they stood completely still. Oi was standing on the conveyor belt, stuffing as many marshmallows into his mouth as he could and doing the most ridiculous dance he had ever done. (He didn't realise it, but he was actually doing the Floss *hundreds* of years before it had been invented.)

'It looks like he's eating it. Yes, that's what he's doing. He's stuffing it in his mouth and eating mouthful after mouthful.' The two guards stared at the boy. It had been a long time since they'd had to deal with an emergency. They couldn't even remember what the first step was in the Evil Army's *What-to-Do-in-an-Emergency Handbook*.

'*Hey! Hey, you! Stop it. Come 'ere!*' The two guards shouted as loudly as they could, but it didn't make any difference. The boy wouldn't stop. He just kept eating and Flossing. More guards joined them.

'What's going on?' they said.

'It's that boy over there. He's stuffing his face with marshmallows.'

'The general's marshmallows?'

'The general's marshmallows.'

'Wait a minute. I think there's another one. Look at that one, in the ragged yellow dress. It's Anna, isn't it? The one who carries the buckets of jelly. She's eating and jumping about all over the place.'

'And over there! Isn't that Jack? He's one of the worst.'

'Another!'

'They're all at it!'

Suddenly, the very bored Evil Army soldiers were no longer very bored. They ran towards the children as fast as they could, waving their swords and daggers. At last they had something fun to do! More soldiers joined them. They charged towards the children, who were spread all over the factory.

Oi watched the chaos. Then he jumped off the conveyor belt and started to run back down the mountain. The rest of the children followed. This was the clever part of Beatrix's plan. You see, the children weren't just running in any old direction, they were running towards Oi, and once they reached Oi they made sure all the soldiers were running together in a big group, which was exactly how Beatrix wanted them.

Meanwhile, Beatrix, Matilda and Wilfred ran in the opposite direction, without any soldiers chasing them, towards the giant saucepan hanging over the fire.

They heaved at the heavy chains, turning the handle to twist the pan. It creaked away from the fire pit, spinning so it was upside down. A few gooey drops of marshmallow fell onto the ground. All they needed now was twenty soldiers to drop it on.

25

Into the River

Oi and the children were running as fast as they could, throwing pieces of marshmallow on the ground to distract the soldiers. The soldiers were a lot faster at running than they expected. The children ran round the entire factory, then into the enormous barn and slammed the doors shut behind them.

The soldiers gathered by the barn doors, getting ready to knock them down. They were out of breath and excited at the thought of capturing the children. You couldn't just eat General Burpintime's marshmallows. No one was allowed to eat them without his permission. And as for throwing them on the ground, the Evil Army soldiers didn't like to think what he'd do to them because of that.

'Right, let's get these doors open,' said one of the soldiers. 'Time to punish some children.'

They were so busy getting ready to charge at the doors that they didn't notice the enormous saucepan hovering above their heads. They didn't hear the creak of the chains as Beatrix and Wilfred got ready to drop it, and they didn't notice the sudden whirring sound as they let go of the chains and it fell to the ground.

They heard the thump of it hitting the snow, and they noticed they could no longer see anything at all. But by then it was too late. They were trapped in the pitch-black pan. For a moment, there was silence. Then there was an almighty din, as twenty

angry soldiers started banging and whacking the sides of the saucepan, trying to get out.

'Excellent!' Beatrix said. 'That's taken care of them. Now we need to get all the children out of the barn, and get those huge pieces of marshmallow down to the river to use as boats.'

She ran to the barn doors, shouting for Oi.

In a moment, the doors swung inwards. The children came out in groups of four, carrying the great big marshmallow mattresses between them to the water's edge. The river was flowing fast, swollen by melted snow. The water looked black and dangerous.

'I'm not sure if this is such a good idea,' Matilda said, looking at the water.

'What are you talking about? It's a brilliant idea!'

Matilda's brother, Jack, was standing next to her, hopping up and down in excitement.

'This is my brother, Jack,' Matilda said.

'Nice to meet you, Jack,' Beatrix said. 'You can be in charge of one of the boats. Just make sure you hold on tight. There's no other way out of the valley so it's got to be the river.' She hoped it would be fine – but if anyone fell off their marshmallow boat they'd end up in ice-cold water, and they wouldn't survive. The current was so fast they'd be pulled under in a second and might get knocked out on the rocks.

'What's going on over there?' Wilfred said. He pointed towards the mountain. 'It looks like lights coming out of the tunnel we came through.'

Beatrix stared in the direction he was pointing. Wilfred was right. Flickering torches were coming out of the tunnel like a swarm of fireflies, charging down the hillside.

'Listen,' Beatrix said. 'Can you hear that?' A stomach-churning chant floated on the still night air:

'*KILL KILL KILL KILL KILL KILL!*'

It echoed round the valley.

'More soldiers!' Beatrix said. 'They must have come from Riddletown, through the secret passage. We've no time to lose. Onto the marshmallow boats.'

As she said this a flaming arrow flew through the air, lighting up the night sky above them.

It landed in the ground a few metres from her, setting fire to a pile of wooden crates. The children around her looked up in astonishment.

'What the?!' Oi said. Overhead the sky was lit up as if it was Bonfire Night, and flaming arrows sped towards them.

'Get under the marshmallows!' Beatrix shouted, running to a group of children and helping them lift one of the marshmallow boats over their heads. 'To the river, quick as you can!'

Everyone ran as fast as they could, holding the giant marshmallow boats over their heads like enormous umbrellas. Occasionally they heard a splat and sizzle, as an arrow plunged into one of the marshmallows. Then came the smell of it toasting.

'Let's get these boats into the river,' Beatrix said. 'Splash water onto them to put out the fires. Then two of you hold onto each one while the others climb on board.'

It was shallow and muddy by the river bank. The shouts of '*KILL KILL KILL!*' were getting louder. They could see shadowy forms running towards them.

Soon, five marshmallow boats, still smoking from the fires that had started on them, were ready to float downriver. The children climbed on board. Matilda was with Jack, both of them holding tightly to the sticky marshmallow. The boats floated towards the centre of the river, where the current was strongest. The children dug their hands into the marshmallow to try to hold on. Oi lifted Dog onto the boat, before sitting down himself and taking out a chunk and eating it.

' 'S good!' he said. 'At least we won't get hungry on the journey.'

'Don't eat the boat, Oi!' Beatrix replied, trying not to feel sick as the marshmallow lurched to the left and the right. 'Once we're in the middle of the river the current will carry us away,' she said.

'Look – on the shore! What on earth…?'
Wilfred said.

They all looked towards the shore. A greenish
shape was lurching through the snow towards
them.

'The dragon!' Matilda said.

26

Help Is On Its Way

'Come back here at once! Come back here or I'll burn all your homes to the ground!' the dragon shouted, in his strange, high-pitched voice.

Then the dragon jumped into the water. Dog was barking like mad. He'd never seen a dragon before, but it definitely looked like something he should chase. Oi struggled to hold on but Dog leapt from his arms into the river, swimming for the shore.

'No!' cried Oi. 'Come back!' Dog had already reached the shallows. 'Stop the boat – we can't float away without Dog!'

Wilfred slid into the icy water, holding onto the marshmallow boat so it didn't get dragged into the middle of the river and pulled downstream with the other boats.

Oi and Beatrix climbed off the boat and waded towards the shore, dodging the flaming arrows that were still flying overhead. '*Dog! Come back!*' they shouted.

'What's that flapping around the dragon's head?' Beatrix said. 'It looks like Jeff!'

Jeff the pigeon was back – and not only was he back, he was diving at the dragon as if he wanted to peck it to pieces.

Dog had reached the dragon too – he was yapping at it and biting its ankles and running in circles around it, splashing about in the shallows with a furious energy.

'Get away from me!' the dragon shouted. It tried to kick Dog but he was too quick, and kept snapping at him. The shallows were muddy, and the dragon found his feet were getting stuck. It was hard to keep his balance. He reached down to grab Dog with both his hands, but as he did so Jeff dived at his head.

'*What on earth…?*' he called out, trying to fight off Jeff.

Dog ran between the dragon's legs and jumped up and bit him as hard as he could on the bottom. The dragon let out an almighty (and not very dragony) scream, then fell forward into the muddy water. No sooner was he down than Dog dived at his head, grabbing the dragon's nose with his teeth and pulling at it as if it was a fallen piñata.

'Dog! What are you doing?! Come back to the boat!' Beatrix and Oi shouted.

Dog chewed and ripped and pulled at the dragon's head until it came clean off the body.

Jeff flew in circles around Dog, then landed on Oi's shoulder.

'Dog just killed the dragon!' Oi shouted. 'He's bitten its head off!'

Dog splashed towards them through the water, pulling the dragon's head behind him. Beatrix grabbed him.

'Back to the boat, quick!' she said, as a flaming arrow zipped through the sky above them, lighting up a very strange scene.

'Is that who I think it is?' Wilfred said. He was still in the water, clinging onto the marshmallow boat, trying to stop it being pulled downstream. His whole body was shaking with cold. Beatrix and Oi turned and looked back at the shore.

'It looks like General Burpintime – well, I mean it looks like General Burpintime crossed with a large green chicken,' Beatrix said, as she climbed back onto the boat.

'It *is* General Burpintime!' Oi said.

Burpintime stood in the water, wearing half a soggy dragon costume and shouting at the top of his voice. He was shaking his fist and punching the air.

'I'M GOING TO DESTROY YOU, BEATRIX THE BOLD, AND I'M GOING TO DESTROY YOUR PALACE, AND I'M GOING TO DESTROY YOUR WHOLE FAMILY IN BELUGA AND YOU'LL NEVER SEE THEM EVER AGAIN! AND I'M GOING TO DESTROY YOUR TOYS. ALL YOUR TOYS. AND THAT DOG THAT'S NOT EVEN YOURS. AND THAT PIGEON. ESPECIALLY THE PIGEON. YOU HEAR ME?'

'I don't think he likes you very much,' Oi said, settling onto the boat.

Wilfred steered the raft back to the middle of the river then jumped back aboard, and the current started to pull them downstream again.

'No. I don't think he does. Who's that next to him?' Beatrix said, looking back over her shoulder.

'It looks like Esmerelda! It is! I can't believe it – she's been helping Burpintime!'

As Wilfred strained his eyes to see, the marshmallow boat floated further away from the madly fizz-popping general.

'You're right. It's her. She really is...'

'Terrible?' Oi said.

'She's worse than terrible,' Beatrix said. 'Next to her, someone who's terrible is actually quite nice. She needs a new name.'

'Esmerelda the Terribly Terrible?' Oi suggested.

'Esmerelda the Worse than Someone Who's Really Terrible?' Wilfred said.

Beatrix frowned. 'More like Esmerelda the Massive Pain in the –' A flaming arrow whooshed overhead and landed with a sizzle in the cold water, drowning out her words.

'Numb Butt Lane?' Oi said.

27

Back to Riddletown

If you've ever been on one of those rides at a theme park where you bounce down a pretend river and get a bit splashed, you'll know exactly how the children on their marshmallow boats were feeling. For the first few minutes it was quite exciting – the rafts swayed this way and that, bouncing off the rocks. Matilda and Jack clung on tightly. For the next few minutes it was less exciting, and a bit more sicky-feeling, as

the river rolled them to the left and to the right, up and down and up and down on the current. After that it was all just sicky feelings. Like being stuck on a never-ending theme-park ride. Made of marshmallow. When you're feeling seasick, the smell of slightly toasted marshmallow is one of the worst smells you can smell.

The children huddled together, feeling cold. The night sky changed from black to grey as the sun rose behind the clouds. As the sky brightened, they could see more of the world around them. The river flowed through fields, still covered in snow. The water was moving more slowly now. In the distance, they could see the smudgy grey outline of Riddletown.

'Looks like we'll be there soon,' Beatrix said. 'Which is good, because if the journey goes on much longer Oi will have eaten a hole in the boat.'

'What?' Oi said, looking up, his mouth full.

'Stop eating the boat. Surely you've had enough marshmallow!'

'There's no such thing as enough marshmallow. And the bits that caught fire taste even better.'

'Hey, Matilda,' Beatrix called out, 'look at this!' She held up the soggy dragon's head. 'No more Riddletown Dragon!'

And Matilda grinned.

The marshmallow boats drifted down the River Riddle into Riddletown. The town was still and silent – the only people up were those on their way to market. As the rafts went under the bridge, people stopped and stared. What were these big white floaty things in the river, covered in children? They were like a new kind of biscuit, the kind an ogre would like to gobble up. They started calling out to them, running down to the river bank.

'*What's going on? What are you doing?!*'

'*Hang on – isn't that Anna? The girl who disappeared last year?*'

'*And her friend, the one who broke my window!*'

'*And isn't that Jack, Matilda's brother?*'

'*Look, there's Matilda too!*'

More people came out of their houses to see what was going on. They threw ropes to the children, pulling the marshmallow boats towards the river bank. By now the whole town was awake.

There was a great commotion as everybody crowded round.

The people of Riddletown were laughing and crying and hugging each other. They had their children back. Matilda tried to find Beatrix so she could thank her and, of course, tell the whole town to thank her, but she was nowhere to be seen. All she found was a soggy dragon's head, sitting on the river bank.

Beatrix, Wilfred and Oi had slipped away through the crowd without anyone noticing. They walked along the narrow streets to where they'd left the cart. Oi and Beatrix climbed onto it, feeling as if they could sleep for a thousand years. It had been the longest night of their lives. Wilfred took hold of the reins and flicked them. The horse made a sleepy *Neeeiiggghhh* sort of noise and the cart trundled off, bouncing over the cobbles in a bottom-achingly bottom-aching end to their adventure.

'Well,' Wilfred said, as they reached the gates of Riddletown, 'that was an adventure I wasn't expecting to have.'

'Me neither,' said Oi. 'But at least we managed to save all those children. I can't imagine how horrible it must have been having to make marshmallow all day and not be able to eat any of it. No one deserves that.'

'We didn't save *all* the children,' Beatrix said, after a moment. 'Matilda told me some had escaped over the years. No one knows where they went or what happened to them. They didn't go back to Riddletown.'

'How strange,' Wilfred said.

'How very strange,' Oi said.

'Woof,' said Dog.

Jeff the pigeon didn't say anything. He just pooped in his cage.

The cart reached the gates. There were no guards – they'd all run to the centre of town to see the children, so there was no riddle to answer. Well, *almost* no riddle. Beatrix still couldn't work out where all the children had gone who'd run away.

It was another mystery, but for now she'd had enough of riddles. Her brain was too tired to try and solve it. She thought instead about her father and mother. Now that she'd reunited the children of Riddletown with their parents, she felt more determined than ever to find her own.

'By the way,' Oi said. 'Do you think we should find a faster way to get to Beluga? It's too late to cross the mountains now – there could be avalanches And the last thing I heard General

 Burpintime say when he was shouting and jumping up and down on the river bank, was something like, *I'M GOING TO DESTROY YOUR WHOLE FAMILY IN BELUGA AND YOU'LL NEVER SEE THEM EVER AGAIN!* I can't be one hundred per cent sure, but it definitely sounded like that.'

'And Esmerelda was standing next to him,' Wilfred said. 'Which means they'll be plotting their next steps already.'

'We'll get to Beluga as fast as we can,' Beatrix replied. 'But it'll mean sailing across the Sea of Sinking Ships. And that means we'll have to hire a ship. And a crew.'

'And not sink,' Oi said.

'Definitely not sink,' said Wilfred. 'It's too far to swim. We'll need to look out for pirates too – I've heard there are pirates in those waters.'

'And sea monsters,' Oi said. 'And terrible storms.'

'Anything else?' Beatrix asked. 'Sea Wobblers? Giant jelly-baby fish? Angry swimming cats? We've just defeated General Burpintime and his army for the second time and freed all those children from a lifetime of marshmallow making. It'll take more than a few pirates and sea monsters and whatever other stories people tell to stop me getting to Beluga.'

28

The End
(well, almost)

And talking of General Burpintime, he was at that very moment standing in front of his boss, the Evil Overlord, trying to explain what had just happened without making himself sound like a complete nincompoop.

Martin and Colin were there too. They stood behind him, still dressed as farmers and looking very sorry for themselves.

General Burpintime hated these meetings.

When he did the right
thing, like winning a
war, the Evil Overlord
was never satisfied.
He'd just ask why he
hadn't won the battle
more quickly. When he did

the wrong thing, like not capturing Beatrix the
Bold, or not capturing Beatrix the Bold again, it
was like standing in front of a tornado that had
got stuck in your living room.

The Evil Overlord had finished screaming and
shouting and was now simply shaking his head
at the general. The general's ears were ringing, as
if he'd been listening to very loud music.

'So you still haven't captured Beatrix the Bold?'
the Evil Overlord said.

'No. I still haven't captured her.'

'Even though she was right next to your castle?'

'Even though she was right next to my castle.'

'And now she's freed all those children you enslaved to make your marshmallows.'

'Yes. She freed all the children.' Burpintime's face twitched when he said this, as if a fly was buzzing round him.

'And she burnt your marshmallow factory to the ground.'

'Yes. Well, not exactly. I…' Burpintime paused. He didn't want to admit that his soldiers had done this when they fired their flaming arrows, or he'd look even more stupid than he already did.

The Evil Overlord shook his head and sighed. Then he shook his head again. Then he sighed. Then he looked at General Burpintime and shook his head. Then he sighed. On his desk was a big red button. Under Burpintime's feet was a trap door. One press of the button, and Burpintime would drop through the floor onto some very sharp metal spikes.

'It's not good enough, is it?' the Evil Overlord said.

'No, it's not.'

'Your father was a famous general, wasn't he? What do you think he'd make of this?'

'I think he'd be very disappointed.'

'I think you're right. He'd be very disappointed indeed.' The Evil Overlord's finger edged closer to the big red button. He stared at General Burpintime.

General Burpintime started talking very quickly, his high voice became even higher:

'I have a plan,' he said.

'What kind of plan?'

'A really, really good plan. We know she's going to see her parents in Beluga, so I'm going to get there first. I'll take over their castle, kidnap her parents, then wait for her to turn up and rescue them,' he said. 'Simple. It'll work. Trust me.'

The Evil Overlord's finger moved slowly away from the red button. He didn't trust anyone.

'It'd better,' he said.

29

One Last Magic Trick

Oh – one *very* last thing: a conversation between Beatrix, Oi and Wilfred as they make their way to the Sea of Sinking Ships. A conversation about an Evil Army knife, and a bottle…

'As far as I can see, the only way you could get the knife in the bottle is if you made the bottle around the knife,' Beatrix said. 'Or maybe you broke the bottom off a bottle, put the knife in, then melted the glass and stuck the bottom back on.'

'And then filled it with beer,' Oi said. 'But you definitely didn't have a glass blower hiding under the table in the squashed-meatball inn. At least not one that I saw. And I didn't see you pouring beer into anything.'

'So that means you'd have had to do all that before we left. Which means you must have already had the knife, which is impossible,' Beatrix added.

Wilfred flicked the horse's reins as the cart trundled along the track towards the Sea of Sinking Ships. He was silent for a moment, then he said:

'Aren't you both forgetting one thing?'

Oi and Beatrix looked at each other, then back at Wilfred.

'I don't think so,' Beatrix replied.

'The possibility that this was *actual* magic?' Wilfred said.

Beatrix and Oi were very still. Beatrix knew this wasn't possible, but all the same…

'Was it?' Oi said.

Wilfred smiled.

'Of course not! I got the dagger from the Evil Army's camp when we disguised ourselves as Wobblers and defeated the Evil Army last year; I got a glass blower to take the bottom off a bottle and stick it back on with the knife inside, and then I filled it with beer. And you're right, I had to carry it with me the whole way, inside my cape, just in case it was needed. Just in case we bumped into Evil Army soldiers. I've still got two emergency tricks in here,' he said, patting his pockets.

Beatrix thought about this. In a way, it was more impressive than actual magic. All you needed for that was a spell and a sort of '*Ta-dah*', combined with a wand wiggle. It didn't take as much effort.

'It takes a lot of work to make someone believe in magic,' Beatrix said.

'Yes, but it's worth it,' Wilfred replied. 'Especially if your life depends on it.'

How to Draw a Dragon

General Burpintime's artist is terrible at drawing people, but very good at drawing marshmallows. He's never tried drawing a dragon, because drawing dragons is DANGEROUS. But just in case you ever want to draw a dragon, there are two ways of doing it.

Method 1:
• Find a dragon (dragons are quite hard to find because they're very shy, but if you look carefully at some very old maps, or indeed Google maps, you might just see *here be dragons* written in small letters in certain far off places).

• Go to one of these places – make sure you tell your mum and dad where you're going, and pack a spare pair of pants, at least two rounds of sandwiches and a fire extinguisher.

• Be very, very quiet. When the dragon appears, draw VERY, VERY quickly.

• If it breathes fire, use the fire extinguisher.

Method 2:
• First draw a giraffe. (A giraffe is the animal that most looks like a dragon. I know there's an animal called a Komodo Dragon, but this looks more like a crocodile, and you don't want to draw a crocodile.)

• Once you've drawn your giraffe, you'll need to make the legs and neck a little shorter, add some wings and a long tail and lots of triangles so it looks scaly. You'll also need to make it look very grumpy. Dragons are a lot more grumpy than giraffes because the fire in their belly gives them tummy ache.

• If you can't draw a dragon (or a giraffe), draw an egg instead and tell everyone there's a dragon inside it.

Quiz

Test your knowledge of the Riddletown Dragon with the quiz below. If you get all the answers right, General Burpintime will give you a carriage full of gold (at least, that's what he told me when I asked him to provide a prize for the quiz).

1. On Beatrix's map there's something that looks like a big bar of chocolate. What is it really?

2. What colour does Oi think the yoke is in a parrot's egg?

3. What does the sign at Matilda's cake stall say?

4. Which months of the year have two 'O's in their name?

5. According to legend, what are conkers actually made from?

6. What's the only vegetable General Burpintime will eat?

7. Scaly dragons breathe fire. What do red-spotted curtain dragons breathe?

8. What cake will you end up looking like if you don't do what General Burpintime says?

9. What's drawn on the walls in the tunnel under the mountain?

10. How many marshmallow boats do they need to escape from the marshmallow factory?

Bonus question: What did one snowman say to the other snowman?

Answers: 1. General Burpintime's castle, 2. Green, 3. No Riddle – No service, 4. October (and Joon and Jooly), 5. Dragon poo, 6. Peas, 7. Paint, 8. A pancake, 9. Children, 10. Five,

Bonus answer: *Can you smell carrots?*

How to Make Sprout Soup

Sprout soup is one of the simplest recipes ever. There are only two ingredients. The first, unsurprisingly, is sprouts. The second is *also* sprouts. The traditional Riddletown recipe for sprout soup is as follows:

1. Boil lots of sprouts in a big pan of hot water
2. Add more sprouts.
3. Mush them all up.
4. Pour the gloopy green mixture into bowls.
5. Eat as quickly as possible while holding your nose.

If you don't like the sound of that, Mrs Fartinpants has another recipe for sprout soup you could try:

1. Boil a big cauldron of water over a fire.
2. Add chicken, bacon, carrots and potatoes and leave to simmer for at least two hours.
3. Add one small sprout.
4. Count five seconds, then remove the sprout.
5. Carefully pour the soup into bowls, carefully put the sprout in the bin. (Or you can add it to one of bowls of soup and hide it under the chicken!)

Acknowledgements

Thanks once again to my agent Chloe and the amazing team at Piccadilly Press for all their support and enthusiasm. To Georgia for keeping the story on the right tacks, to Jenny for attention to detail and to Cherie for creating another fantastic cover and such wonderful illustrations. Thanks also to Louis for listening to first drafts, re-drafts and ridiculous riddles, and Penelope, without whom Beatrix would not exist.

Don't miss Beatrix's next adventures in *Beatrix the Bold and the Balloon of Doom!*

Beatrix the Bold is on the run from the Evil Army *and* her evil aunt Esmerelda, but she's getting closer to finding her long-lost parents, whom she hasn't seen since she was a baby. She just has to cross the Sea of Sinking Ships and the Volcanos of Doom to get to them. But when you're Beatrix the Bold and you've got Oi the boy, Dog the dog and Wilfred the Wise by your side, you can do *anything...*

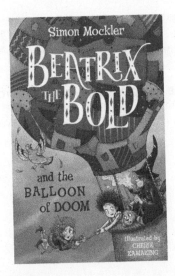

P R E S S

Thank you for choosing a Piccadilly Press book.

If you would like to know more about our
authors, our books or if you'd just like to know
what we're up to, you can find us online.

www.piccadillypress.co.uk

And you can also find us on:

We hope to see you soon!